Elizabeth A. F. H. Le Blond

High Life

and Towers of Silence

Elizabeth A. F. H. Le Blond

High Life
and Towers of Silence

ISBN/EAN: 9783337168452

Printed in Europe, USA, Canada, Australia, Japan

Cover: Foto ©Andreas Hilbeck / pixelio.de

More available books at **www.hansebooks.com**

HIGH LIFE

AND

TOWERS OF SILENCE

BY THE AUTHOR OF

"THE HIGH ALPS IN WINTER; OR, MOUNTAINEERING IN SEARCH
OF HEALTH"

London

SAMPSON LOW, MARSTON, SEARLE, & RIVINGTON

CROWN BUILDINGS, 188, FLEET STREET

1886

TO

EDOUARD CUPELIN,

OF CHAMONIX,

the guide who accompanied me in most of my wanderings, and to whose pluck and knowledge of his work I owe whatever success I achieved in the excursions which we made together,

I DEDICATE THIS VOLUME.

PREFACE.

MESSIEURS LES INTRÉPIDES !

If, in the hope of reading accounts of Alpine
ascents, you honour me by glancing at this volume,
you will find on page 65 the only record of
climbing likely to interest you, if you search for
novelty.

But, if you care to wander with me over familiar
ground, and amongst familiar faces, perhaps I may
be able to give you a few hours' pleasure as, one
by one, the well-known scenes rise up before you.

Switzerland is thronged with our compatriots in
summer, and is visited by many of them in winter
also ; I must, therefore, beg the indulgence of my
readers if I tell them much which it is possible
they know already, and if I often tread with them
over "les grandes voies où l'humanité a passé."

The public, who received with such undeserved

kindness my first work, will, I feel sure, extend their good will to this also, and will understand my difficulty in trying to represent familiar scenes under new aspects.

ELIZABETH MAIN.

SAAS-FÉE,
July, 1886.

CONTENTS.

CHAPTER I.

SOME WINTER SCENES IN SWITZERLAND.

CHAPTER II.

TOURISTS AND OTHERS WHOM ONE MEETS.

CHAPTER V.

THE FLOODS OF 1882 IN AUSTRIA AND NORTHERN ITALY.

CHAPTER VI.

COL DU TOUR IN SPRING, WITHOUT GUIDES.

CHAPTER VII.

FIRST ASCENT OF THE BIESHORN (13,652 FEET).

A few words about the peaks of the Alps which remained

CHAPTER VIII.

OVER THE MATTERHORN FROM VISP TO BREUIL, AND
BACK TO ZERMATT BY THE ST. THÉODULE WITHOUT
SLEEPING OUT.

CHAPTER IX.

THIRD ASCENT OF THE HIGHEST POINT OF THE DENT
DU GÉANT.

CHAPTER XII.

TWO OLD FRIENDS.

CONCLUSION.

ILLUSTRATIONS.

THE WIESENER ALP IN WINTER

ERRATA.

Page 89, line 13, *for* from the floods, *read* from the land of floods.

„ 149, „ 23, *for* often found between a glacier and a moraine, *read* generally found across the lower end of a couloir.

One of our countrymen starts from Chur for the Engadine—Churwalden recommends itself to the English in an amusing pamphlet—Luncheon at Lenz—Tiefenkasten and its church—The conductor of the post recounts his adventures—He also mentions an ascent of Piz Julier in winter—I digress in order to describe this excursion—A few words about Pontresina guides—We set out for Piz Julier—An avalanche is

B

CHAPTER XII.

TWO OLD FRIENDS.

THE WIESENER ALP IN WINTER.

HIGH LIFE

AND

TOWERS OF SILENCE.

CHAPTER I.

SOME WINTER SCENES IN SWITZERLAND.

Erroneous ideas about winter in the heights of Switzerland—
One of our countrymen starts from Chur for the
Engadine—Churwalden recommends itself to the
English in an amusing pamphlet—Luncheon at Lenz—
Tiefenkasten and its church—The conductor of the
post recounts his adventures—He also mentions an
ascent of Piz Julier in winter—I digress in order to
describe this excursion—A few words about Pontresina
guides—We set out for Piz Julier—An avalanche is

B

started—We reach the summit of the mountain—A long
halt on the rocks—We descend—Upset from a sledge—
The relief party—St. Moritz at last—The typical traveller,
who has rested at the hospice on the Julier, reaches
his destination.

I HAVE been so often questioned with regard to
winter travelling in the high-lying and remote parts
of Switzerland, that perhaps it may interest my
readers if I tell of some of my winter journeys.

On returning to England, after a winter spent in
one of the Alpine health resorts, I am invariably
assailed with such questions as these :—

"Can you leave your winter-quarters once the
snow has fallen ?"

"Are there diligences in which it is possible to
travel from place to place ?"

"Do you get food and letters with regularity ?"

"Can you walk, or must you always remain in
the house ?"

In answer to such queries I will begin by
describing the manner in which an English traveller
arriving at Chur, say, the middle or end of Novem-
ber, is conveyed over the Julier Pass to St. Moritz,
in the Engadine. After a night spent at Chur,
our countryman goes at 7 a.m. to the Post. There

he sees a heavy yellow vehicle, much the same as those used in summer, except that there is no banquette, the accommodation consisting only of the four inside places and the coupé.

He wonders how this clumsy conveyance, mounted on high wheels, and drawn by four horses, will force its way through the snow which, he hears, already lies thickly on the Julier Pass. There is only a thin sprinkling on the ground at Chur, though the surrounding hills are already clothed in their heavy winter garb.

At last all the luggage is hoisted up on the top of the diligence, the conductor has snugly en-sconced himself alone in the interior, with both windows closed, thus, after a time, securing, on this hot and sunny day, a temperature something akin to that of his living-room at home; the driver cracks his whip, and the vehicle moves off, and soon begins laboriously to mount the long incline to Churwalden. The traveller, from his place in the coupé, notices that the patches of snow on the road are becoming larger and more frequent, till, at last, everything is shrouded in white. Every few minutes one of the wheels of the diligence sinks deeply into a small drift, and the vehicle lurches over on one side, a performance somewhat disquieting to persons of weak nerves and lively imaginations. Churwalden is the next village of considerable size above Chur. It is resorted to in summer by Swiss and a few English. A pamphlet recommending the place contains the curious statement that "Churwalden has become an airing-place," and the document is signed, "Dr. DENZ, physician, living at the Kurhaus, and owning an apothecary's shop."

Arrived at Churwalden, our friend is told to alight. On doing so he sees, drawn up near the Post, two or three sledges, painted yellow and black. Each is intended to hold two persons, and has a board at the back on which the driver stands. There is also a sledge for the luggage, and each of the sledges is drawn by one horse.

Some country folk are waiting for the diligence to take them to Lenz. One of them is put into a sledge with our English traveller, two more go together, and the fourth in the remaining sledge with the conductor. Our countryman thinks that the moving of the luggage from the large diligence to the sledge is a very tedious affair, and he wonders how soon they will be ready to start. At last an individual in the regulation blue coat and shiny hat appears. " Now," thinks our friend, " here is the driver, so we shall soon be off." However, to his surprise, after taking hold of the reins, the driver does not seem as if he intends to use them On the contrary, he ties them in many and curious loops round the horse's neck, a proceeding which the traveller cannot as yet understand. Having finished his apparently aimless task, the driver leads the horse out into the road, where two of the sledges are already standing. The horse who is to draw the luggage has his reins also arranged round his neck, and the driver having got all the sledges in line, the conductor first, the Englishman second, himself standing at the back of the third, and the baggage at the end, he cries, " Vorwärts ! " cracks his whip and flicks it along the line, and the procession starts. It has now become clear to our traveller that the next stage of his journey is to be made in a sledge without a driver ! He tries to question his companion, but cannot understand any of the peasant's vile Grisons patois, mumbled out between puffs of viler Grisons tobacco. The train of sledges

mounts the slope at a quick walk—the pace is
decidedly faster than it would be in summer. Arriving at the summit of the Lenzerhöhe, a widely
stretching heath at the top of the pass between
Chur and Tiefenkasten, the horses break into a
trot, and in a short time the town of Lenz is reached.
Here less snow is found, the sledges grind over the
stones in the paved streets, and stop at the Post,
where a large yellow diligence stands, similar to that
left at Churwalden. A halt is made at·Lenz for
luncheon, and the traveller is ushered upstairs to a
room, in which stands a long table with two places
laid at one end of it.

"For whom is the second place?" wonders our
friend. Switzerland is a Republic, and we are constantly reminded of that fact in various ways. One
man is as good as another here—or a great deal
better, as the conductor of the diligence, who now
strides in, no doubt thinks, judging from the
patronizing way in which he nods to our countryman, and, seating himself opposite, passes the veal-
cutlets after first helping himself! A kindly, brave
man he is, all the same, and, when battling with a
snowstorm on an Alpine Pass, the weary and half

Chapel containing Skulls and Bones.

frozen travellers, who may be with him, will certainly
find it out.

The somewhat greasy and comfortless meal
concluded, the journey is resumed once more, this
time on wheels. A steep descent leads to Tiefenkasten, where those who find the drive from Chur
to the Engadine too long for one day, sometimes
spend the night. Tiefenkasten is a Roman Catholic
village, and an inspection of the church will repay
those who have not already visited similar places
of worship in out-of-the-way parts of Switzerland.
At the gate leading to the church, to right and left,
are two small chapels. Looking through the bars
of the gate closing the entrance of that to the
right, we see a figure resembling those carried in
procession on the festival of Corpus Christi, in
Roman Catholic districts. This figure is of white
plaster, and kneeling around it are numerous other
figures carved in brown wood, which look sorrowfully
towards the recumbent figure in their midst. An
altar stands behind, and above it a statue of the
Virgin and Child. All the figures are nearly life-
size, and, in spite of the roughness of the work-
manship and the neglected state of the chapel, the

sight is much more impressive than would be imagined. In the other chapel, on the left of the gateway, is kept the collection of skulls and bones, found in all the parishes of this district. They are piled up on the floor, and numbered. An altar also stands in this chapel with two large figures above it ; one of these is in brown wood, and represents a soul in torments, with its hands clasped and flames rising around it, The other, which is in plaster and coloured, is intended for the Virgin Mary, who turns away from the imploring figure at her side. The church itself does not contain much of interest, though, if visited early in the morning, the stranger will no doubt notice the fine effect produced by the sun shining through the two upper windows at the east end.

Leaving Tiefenkasten, the road mounts steadily to Mühlen, and again the tedious process of transferring the luggage from the wheeled vehicle to the sledge is performed. The traveller is glad to find that the conductor, who will drive his sledge, is to be his only companion, while the luggage is in charge of the driver. Within the last two years a closed sledge crosses the Julier Pass in winter when the road is in good order, but on windy days, and after fresh snow, small open sledges must be used.

The conductor has many tales of adventure, which he much enjoys relating. He tells how, on stormy days in winter, he has crossed the Albula or Flucla passes, famous for their avalanches. He describes the difficulties of advancing against the raging wind, which sweeps up the powdery snow and dashes it furiously into the eyes of horses and travellers, while the poor animals flounder in the drifts which completely cover the track. Sometimes, in spite of the skill of the driver, the sledge slips over the side of the track and down the slope. In this case it is a matter of time and difficulty once more to regain the road, but, with the aid of the roadmen, who accompany the post in bad weather, it is at length accomplished.

Again, it is not unfrequent to come upon a huge avalanche which has fallen a short time previously and completely blocked the track. The only thing to be done, under these circumstances, is to wait for the coming of the diligence from the other side. On its arrival, the luggage is lifted over the mass of snow, the travellers scramble across after it, and each conveyance returns to the point from which it started.

With many such exciting tales, made none the less thrilling by constant repetition (in fact, the size of an avalanche will grow till one wonders that the end of it does not reach Chur), the time is whiled away, the last dull slopes mounted and the dreary summit of the Pass reached.

When crossing this Pass a couple of years ago I was much entertained by hearing the conductor relate how an Englishwoman had been nearly killed, a month or two previously, in company with a German and two guides, while ascending Piz Julier, the fine peak rising upwards of 11,000 feet above the sea, to the left of the Pass when it is approached from Chur.

While the post halts at the dingy little inn on the Pass, and during the time passed by the traveller in trying to swallow some most uninviting coffee, and by the horses in nibbling the hard, black bread of the country, let me briefly describe our ascent of Piz Julier (for I was the Englishwoman spoken of by the conductor). Had some of us been killed, the narrative would, no doubt, have much increased in interest; but as we certainly were in peril of our lives, it is the next best thing to having lost them, so far as supplying a point for this story is concerned.

I had been told that, up to the time of our excursion, Piz Julier had not been ascended in winter, but I learnt afterwards that a party had been up it some years before at that season, and were, for a considerable time, in much danger from avalanches.

A few words before I relate our experiences on Piz Julier, with regard to our choice of guides.

At the beginning of January in that same year I wished to ascend Piz Roseg. Hans Grass of Pontresina would have been willing to accompany me, and I much regretted that an injury to his knee, which he had sustained the previous summer, rendered it impossible for him to undertake so long an excursion.

His nephew, Christian, would also have gladly joined our party, but, unfortunately, he was then at Davos, fulfilling the less exciting duties of concierge to the Buol Hotel.

All the other Pontresina guides refused to climb in winter, fearing to risk their precious necks and unintelligent heads at that season. I received plenty of letters from some of them, who at first decided to go, but excused themselves at the last moment, containing elaborate references to avalanches, frost-bites, wives, and children.

When, therefore, I realized the scarceness of stout hearts in Pontresina, I telegraphed for my guide from Chamonix, Edouard Cupelin, and finding two St. Moritz men, Colani and Schocher by name, who were willing to accompany us, we made the ascent on the 11th of January, 1884, of the Schneekuppe of Piz Roseg. The weather broke immediately afterwards, so Cupelin returned home.

About ten days later I started with a German friend and the same two local guides, for Piz Julier. We left St. Moritz at 5 a.m. in a sledge, drove to within three-quarters of an hour of the Julier Pass, and, alighting, began the ascent of some toilsome, snow-covered slopes, subsiding every few minutes into concealed rhododendron bushes and holes, which had formed between boulders. Our progress was slow, but we were steadily rising, and distant summits came, one by one, into view, for the day was cloudless and the sky free from all haze. At last, after mounting a gully, in which the snow was soft and powdery, and ready to slide away at any moment in a hissing stream, we emerged at the commencement of a rather steep and wide spur. I must now describe, as minutely as possible, the position in which we found ourselves.

Schocher, who led, was standing at the base of a snow-slope, the width of which was perhaps twenty feet. I was by his side, and Colani a few feet to the left, while my German friend, Mr. H., was still in the gully, up the last part of which he was struggling with the snow nearly to his waist. He was occasionally encouraged by a chuck of the rope from Colani, which had the effect of altogether upsetting his equilibrium and making him more uncomfortable than ever. Behind Schocher and me, and about four feet from us, a precipice fell away to a depth of 300 feet or more, and, on our right, was a very steep gully, while, to our left, was the passage up which we had come.

We were thus on a small and sloping bracket,
waiting for Mr. H., and watching his progress,
when an ominous crack made us all glance
quickly upwards. "The Avalanche!" Colani exclaimed. At that instant we saw a long and ever-
widening slit high above us across the snow, and,
immediately afterwards, felt a heavy pressure
against our knees. Instinctively we leant with
all our weight on our axes. It cannot have been
more than a second or two, yet it seemed ages
till a roar from below like thunder told us that the
avalanche had split longitudinally, and that the
greater part of it had dashed down the gully to
our right. The rest lay round us in blocks, show-
ing the thickness of the crust, which had fairly
peeled off the slope to a depth of several feet.
Colani was trembling and looked as if he could
hardly stand ; Schocher was cool and composed,
and stood quietly waiting for orders ; Mr. H. was
just emerging with one final plunge from his
gully, and wanting to know "what was that noise,"
and if anything was the matter. We were tied
to a rope ninety feet in length. Detaching ourselves, we told Schocher carefully to mount the

slope and anchor himself to the rocks above.
Much of the snow above the place where it had
cracked, was still undisturbed, and one person,
moving through it, was less likely to bring it down
than if we had all gone together. Besides, even if
some of it did get dislodged, we could quickly
draw in the rope and prevent Schocher from being
carried down far with it. He reached the rocks
in safety, and we joined him, one by one, holding
the rope, which stretched from him to us. From
the rocks we reached the summit without further
difficulty in about half an hour.

The view was magnificent. Monte Rosa, pink
in the far distance, was perfectly defined with
its line of well-remembered peaks, and range
after range of familiar mountains could be seen.
The air was warm and still; but on Piz Corvatsch
we could see the snow blown in clouds by the
wind, and we felt sure that a party of friends who
were then ascending that peak, must be suffering
greatly from the cold, as, indeed, on our return, we
heard had been the case. From St. Moritz we
knew that a telescope was directed towards us,
and that our arrival on Piz Julier had been already

observed. While having luncheon, we held a
solemn conclave to decide in what manner our
safe descent was to be accomplished. The result
of the deliberations of the party was something to
this effect: "It's a hot day; two hours ago, when
it was cooler than it is now, we started an avalanche
on a slope which was not particularly steep. If we
begin to descend at once, in an hour or less we
shall reach the beginning of the gully filled with
powdery snow. The sun was off it when we came
up, but, by the time we reach it, it will have been
exposed to great heat for two hours, consequently
we are pretty sure to have an avalanche there.
What will be our wisest way of avoiding this danger
in the descent?" All agreed that the one safe
course to pursue was to remain, as long as possible,
on the summit, and then, going down to the
beginning of the gully, wait till it had been sufficiently long in the shade for the snow to harden a
little.

I need not describe our descent. We followed
out our programme, and, at 5 p.m., when we
should have been at home had all gone well, we
began to go down the gully. At 8.30 p.m. we

reached the high-road. Our sledges had already returned to St. Moritz. We had seen them as we sat on the rocks, two black dots on the white road, which, after waiting some hours, had slowly crawled away. We found walking on a good road a very pleasant change after stumbling through soft snow and creeping down gullies by the light of a candle in a bottle, which invariably contrived to go out, just as one was engaged in taking a particularly long, and especially slippery, downward step, causing one to pause in a cramped position half way, and the man below to miscalculate the length of rope, and pull one down while one grasped one's axe more tightly, and prodded the guide instead of the ice slope.

After walking along the road for some time, the sound of bells was heard, and a rough sledge came up. We accepted the driver's offer of a lift to Silvaplana, and arranged ourselves as well as we could on the primitive conveyance. Soon we were gliding down the zigzags, but, at one of the corners, the driver missed his way in the darkness, and drove off the road. Over went the sledge, and out we shot, up to our necks in the

C

powdery snow. We scrambled out again, none
the worse for our tumble, but in a somewhat irri-
table frame of mind, and were vainly endeavouring
to remove some objectionable particles of snow,
which seemed inclined permanently to take up
their abode between our collars and our necks,
when a jingling of many bells was heard. The
new arrivals turned out to be a search-party from
St. Moritz, consisting of Herr Peter Badrutt, of
the Kulm Hotel, and several guides. These good
people were determined to be ready for all emer-
gencies. They had long iron poles with hooks at
the ends, with which to poke for us in the avalanches, and drag us out if discovered therein.
They had six bottles of brandy, with which to
restore us after the operation just mentioned.
They had yards upon yards of rope wherewith to
lower the party over precipices, with what object
it would be difficult to say. I believe also that
they had a fog-horn, and I am not sure that their
life-saving apparatus did not include a cornet,
belonging to a visitor at the Kulm, who was in
the habit of enlivening his neighbours with sweet
strains from that instrument. It would really have

been interesting to have heard the search-party
signalling to each other, and to have seen the
energy they would have displayed in poking their
iron poles into snow-drifts, and triumphantly pulling
out part of a rhododendron bush ! However, they
were very glad to see us safe and sound. At
11 p.m. we arrived at St. Moritz, and found many
of the household still up. Much anxiety had
been felt on our account. As we were seen on the
summit at an early hour in the day, our friends
expected our return between four and five o'clock
in the afternoon, and the delay seemed inexpli-
cable, except on the supposition that an accident
had happened to us.

But we must now go back to our traveller, who
is getting into his sledge on the Julier Pass. The
drive down-hill is very enjoyable after crawling up
from Mühlen. After a time he can see the road as
it winds below, and on it he notices a number of
black dots, moving quickly along. What can they
be ? He questions the conductor, and that individual, who knows a word or two of English,
answers " toboggans." Our friend hopes that soon
they may overtake them, but, long before the post

reaches Silvaplana, the party of tobogganers are
already there, and when he next sees them, they
are tying their toboggans to the back of their
sledges, and are about to start for St. Moritz.   In
an hour or less the post reaches that little village,
which is the traveller's destination.   He is put
down at the post, and is soon following his luggage, which is being pushed up on a sledge to the
Kulm.

ST. MORITZ IN WINTER

CHAPTER II.

TOURISTS AND OTHERS WHOM ONE MEETS.

Americans abroad—Paterfamilias interviews an *intrépide*—
A party of Americans visit Montanvert—They question
me about the Mer de Glace—Preparations for crossing
the glacier—Americans at the Grands Mulets—I am
warned not to ascend Mont Blanc—The kindly but
tactless person—The stingy and mean person—The
unsnubbable person—The elderly spinster—The person
who always likes to be learning something—The "personally conducted"—The two species of lady climbers
—The German who vindicates the honour of his country
—The intelligent German—The German who speaks a
little English—The spiritual and medical advisers—
Influence of resident doctors over their patients—
Spring quarters—Seewis.

DURING the winter, in such of the Swiss hotels
and pensions as are frequented at that season, we
meet, as a rule, only the health-seeking portion of
our countrymen and of other nations, but in summer the tourist class may be studied at leisure.

As we stand on the long balcony which runs round two sides of the Angleterre at Chamonix, the conversation of a party of typical Americans may often be heard. It is not unfrequently in this style.

Paterfamilias, standing with his hands in his pockets surveying the view, observes that *Mount Blank* does not look so tall as he expected.

"Tall!" cries the eldest hope of that family, "I should think not! Why I could go to the top in two hours!"

Paterfamilias here remarks that the person at the other end of the balcony, who is receiving such glances of admiration from the female portion of the company, in consequence of his recent feat of having his limp form pulled to the summit of the mountain in question, has informed him that "one must sleep at the *Grand Mullets* on the way."

"You mean the *Grand Muleys*, don't you, sir?" says a youth from 'Igh 'Ackney who considers himself to be of an intelligent turn of mind, and who does not object to impart some of his culture to others.

"Stranger!" Paterfamilias exclaims, "I always

mean what I say ; and if I remark that you are
an impertinent Britisher, I mean it ! "

The youth is diminutive and weak-looking. He
scowls darkly at the well-built American, and observing, " I fail to comprehend your allusion ! "
retires from the contest.

" I thought I'd sampled *him* ! " says Paterfamilias complacently, as he saunters along the
balcony and seats himself beside the hero of the
hour.

" Now, tell me, sir," he asks, " is there a good
hotel on the top of *Mount Blank ?* "

The *intrépide* replies with ill-disguised scorn,
that not only is there no building of any
sort on the summit, but that the so-called inn of
the Grands Mulets is a miserable hovel ; that, after
spending the night there, you must start in the
dark with a lantern, climbing over mile after mile
of snow, and that, by the time you have been
hauled up the Bosses, have reached the summit
and have retraced your steps to Chamonix, you
are in a condition of such extreme exhaustion,
that even the roar of the seven-inch long cannons
which are fired in your honour as you proudly

enter the hotel, hardly suffices to revive you. The American is deeply impressed by this account, and exclaims, " Sir ! allow me to shake the hand of so courageous a mountaineer !" which request is promptly complied with, and if the *ascenseur* (I cannot call him a climber), is of a particularly generous turn of mind, perhaps a dirty bit of rag torn from a flag, placed on the summit a few days previously, is offered and gratefully accepted.

See this same family next morning as they wend their way on a string of mules towards what they are pleased to call *Mount Vert*. I remember once, when I was staying there, witnessing the arrival of·such a party. I was having my luncheon at a little table in a distant part of the dining·room, when they entered it, and, after ordering something to eat, they began to look round them. I was both surprised and puzzled to find that, after a few minutes, their glances were unmistakably and exclusively directed towards my corner, and much whispering went on, of which I was evidently the subject. Presently, one of the ladies of the party appeared to take upon herself the weight of a heavy responsibility, for, amid the approving nods of her friends, she came across the room to where I was sitting, and addressed me as follows:—

"Madam, will you be so very kind as to inform me if you have made your face as it is now by crossing the *glacier* this morning ? Because, if our faces are likely to get so blistered and burnt, I guess we won't go over ! "

I replied that I had blistered my face on the Dent du Géant the day before ; whereupon, my questioner wanted to know if that was as bad as the Mer de Glace, and if I thought that if she and her sisters wore three gauze veils, one over the other, their complexions would escape. I fancy that they completely exhausted the supply of veils at the Montanvert bazaar, for, in default of a large enough stock of dark blue, all colours were called into requisition, the temporary disfigurement of appearing in an apple-green veil over two others of blue and yellow (the latter suspiciously like a promoted butterfly net), being as nothing when compared to the horror of having to appear at *table d'hôte* with a skin like mine.

On reaching the edge of the glacier, an individual with a stock of woollen socks, of broken English and of insinuating manners, is generally to be found. He marks out the confiding party of Americans as his prey, and hastens to tell them that, unless they each put on a pair of woollen socks over their boots, they must certainly fall during the slippery passage of the Mer de Glace. He appeals to the guides who may, or may not, be his relations, and these worthies invariably return the answer, which they keep for occasions when the question arises as to the spending or not spending of a certain number of francs, that "it is certainly more prudent." Thereupon, the tourists sit down in a row, and have their boots covered with grey woollen socks, which will, by the time they reach the Chapeau, be hanging in draggled fringes all round their high-heeled French boots. On arriving at that little inn, they have a long inscription burnt into their alpenstocks as a record of their travels, and I heard an American, on one occasion, giving minute directions for the words "London" and "Paris" to head the list.

I recollect another amusing incident connected with this nation. Several years ago, when staying at Chamonix, I met three young Americans, who intended making the ascent of Mont Blanc. They had done no walking previously, but they attached no importance to that fact, and made their plans for going up Mont Blanc, with all the certainty of getting there, which they would have felt regarding a walk to Montanvert, or over what they sometimes call "the Jemmy" (Gemmi). They started in high spirits one lovely morning in July, after giving strict orders that the cannons were to be fired both when they reached the summit, and on their return. For the benefit of those of my readers who have not assisted at this ceremony, I may here add that each hotel has two or three very diminutive cannons, which are fired by the respective porters, who give a prod with a long stick, and then turn and run, while a majestic puff, about the size of an egg, is seen to emerge from the mouth of these warlike machines, followed by a report resembling that of a pistol.

I happened the next day to go up to the Grands Mulets, intending, on the day following, to ascend Mont Blanc. A short time after arriving at the hut, I was informed by Madame Tairraz that there were three gentlemen in the next room who wished to speak to me, and that they were obliged to ask me to come to them as they felt too ill to move.   I accordingly accompanied her into the adjoining room, where I saw three prostrate forms, stretched on three mattresses, and recognized the three aspiring Americans.

"Madam," said No. 1, "we *consider* it our duty to warn you.   We started from here this morning to ascend *Mount Blank*.   We walked over the snow hour after hour.   At length it began to get soft, and we floundered along up to our waists.   Our guides pulled and pulled, and we struggled on for ten weary hours.   Then we asked our guides how much further it was to the summit?   They replied that we were not yet at the Bosses.   We asked "what is the Bosses?"   They answered by pointing upwards to a ridge, about as wide as the blade of a knife, and about as steep as the side of a house.   We thereupon decided that our friends at Chamonix would be very anxious if we did not return in good time, so down we came, and here we are.   Madam," he continued, feebly thumping the mattress with his fist; "madam, no woman can go up *Mount Blank* in all this fresh snow, or no man either, as far as that goes!"

I thanked the American, who was evidently fully persuaded of the accuracy of his statements, sympathized with him on his disappointment in not reaching the top (though I daresay he did so by the time he returned to America), and withdrew. We sneaked through the village next evening to avoid any well-meant salutations from the cannon, and went up to Montanvert, so I did not see our friends again.

Less clever and amusing than our American cousins, but often affording considerable entertainment, is the extraordinary medley of our own country-folk whom we meet in Switzerland.

There is the kindly person—more often than not a clergyman—who gets up parties of uncongenial people, and despatches them on various excursions for which about half of them are totally unfitted. He says to A.: "There is B., who is going to the Jardin to-morrow; why don't you go with him?" "I don't know Mr. B.," replies A. "Then I'll introduce you. Here, Mr. B., is Mr. A., who wants to go to the Jardin to-morrow; you could make the excursion very pleasantly together!" The two men smile a ghastly smile, but there is no way out of it, so A., who weighs eighteen stone suffers from his heart, and likes to take his time over a walk, and B., who has already had a month in Switzerland, is in first-rate training, and is also most anxious to be home in time for dinner, so that he may take pretty Miss C. and her mamma for a walk afterwards, are linked together, and a day's pleasure has many a fetter fastened to it for which neither of the party bless their kind old friend in their inmost hearts.

Then there is the stingy and mean person who, when asked if he will pay for his guide's lunch at Montanvert, invariably answers that he's not going to be cheated into paying what it's not his duty to pay. When taking a room at the Hotel Mont Cervin at Zermatt, he informs Mr. Seiler that he will have to go to another hotel, if he does not get it for less, and sometimes *does* try the other hotels, to the secret merriment of Seiler, who owns them all.   This person occasionally distributes copies of " *The British Workman* " to mule-drivers and others instead of tips, thus arousing evil passions in the hearts of the recipients, but a sense of good works and economy in his own. He furtively takes rolls from the breakfast-table

and puts them in his pocket, where, possibly, they
assimilate with a collection of candle-ends from
the last hotel, and, when the passages are heated,
leaves his door open with the hope of exchanging,
without paying for it, the cold air in his room for
the warm air outside.

We have all encountered the unsnubbable person,
but this individual is met with so constantly in all
countries, and in every class of society, that he is
but too familiar an object to us, and our only wish
is to avoid and forget him.

Then there is the elderly spinster who makes a
point of bringing all her oldest garments to
Switzerland. She does not mind how unsuitable
they may be for travelling. She will boldly mount
a mule in a dress of some thin, flimsy material,
trimmed with lace more or less white. When she
gets down, she leaves a portion of this garment on
the pommel, and various fringes and threads from
the lace may be discovered on the rocks of the
Mauvais Pas after she has crossed it. Her old kid
gloves have no tops to the fingers, and the artificial
flowers in her hat are weatherbeaten by many a
storm. She always wears a bonnet on Sundays

and a mantle from which the greater part of the jet beads, with which it was trimmed, have disappeared.

Then there is the person who is always trying to accumulate masses of information, which is of no use to him, as he never either makes notes of it or remembers it. Every one he meets must answer as many questions as he can manage to ask during the conversation. What is the name of that river? Where does it go to? How long is it? How deep is it? Is it spring or glacier water? Are there many fish in it? What fish? Does one get them at *table d'hôte?* Is one allowed to catch them? What must one use to catch them with? Are they large or small? and so on, without end.

We also meet the party of English or Americans, who are "personally conducted" by an agent of Messrs. Cook or Gaze. This flock is renowned for its absolute helplessness. None of the troop speak a word of any language but their own, so they are continually worrying their unhappy conductor to translate various notices of no possible interest to them, and he is driven nearly wild by their perpetual requests for small change and their complaints as to their accommodation.

"Mr. Smith," says a damsel from across 'The Herring-pond,' "will you lend me twenty-five centimes? I've forgotten my purse." Mr. Smith is just in the act of arranging for the thirty-three mules, which he has chartered for the day, and settling the knotty point as to the just amount to be distributed in tips to the various mule drivers. He hands her the twenty-five centimes, and takes out with a groan, for about the fiftieth time that day, his bulky note-book. Hardly has he finished entering her debt into it than an elderly spinster of forbidding aspect marches up to him. His heart sinks, for he sees trouble ahead. "Mr. Smith," she begins, "I must beg of you not to have me placed at dinner this evening next to Miss A., and I wish to inform you that I will never go on excursions in the same carriage with that young person. If I were you, Mr. Smith, I should consider it my duty to remonstrate with her on her flippant behaviour yesterday morning; why, I heard her asking Mr. B. to come over and sit by her at meals, because she felt sure he was terribly bored by the old frump next him. He sits between me and Mrs. C." (a very popular and comfortable

D

looking old lady), "so I suppose she meant her, which was very ungrateful of the pert little thing, for Mrs. C. has always been friendly to her. Yes, Mr. Smith, it is clearly your duty, for the credit of Mr. Cook's tours, to speak your mind to Miss A."

Mr. Smith shudders. He has a sneaking admiration for Miss A., though her sharp tongue, combined with her pretty face, gets him not unfrequently into trouble. He informs Mrs. C. that he will not throw her and Miss A. more into each other's society than he can help, and he hurries off to see why Mr. D. is beckoning to him with such energy.

" Mr. Smith, come here! Now, do tell this man that I won't be cheated! I've told him that he's asking twice too much for this stick, and I'm sure it's not a real chamois' horn at the top, is it? Please get it for me at a reasonable price, and tell him that I'll never buy anything from him again!"

I could fill pages with such conversations, heard day after day in front of the Montanvert and the Angleterre, at Chamonix, but I fear to become as tedious to my readers as the majority of the personally conducted ones rapidly become to their leader.

Again, we meet the lady climber, who reaches the summits of her peaks, and is usually favoured by the weather. And we meet the other species of lady climber, who either sees the Italian lakes from the summit of the Matterhorn, or against whom all the winds of heaven are ranged, and who encounters a gale, impossible to withstand, on one part of the Weisshorn ridge, while another party is basking in a hot sun and still air a little higher up. This class comprises persons of vine-gary temperament, given to having the tents in which they sleep out blown away, and very critical as to the achievements of other lady climbers, by reason of the fact that they have failed to imitate them. These persons generally find that the best guides, with whom they have climbed once or twice, are doing a wonderfully good business, judging from their numerous engagements. One of these would-be lady climbers may be heard innocently expressing her surprise that there is not a single first-rate guide disengaged for the next day.

" Have you tried so and so ? " inquires a friend.

" Oh, yes," she answers; " he told me this morning that he is engaged for to-morrow."

" Dear me! that is very curious," remarks a bystander, whose first season it is, but whose activity and genial disposition are a delight to the guides, " why I asked him not ten minutes ago if he would ascend the Dom with me to-morrow, and he said he would."

The lady climber is puzzled, but the truth suddenly flashes across the mind of the last speaker, and he feels that he would be glad to have withheld his remark.

Perhaps some of us are familiar with the German, who always vindicates the honour of his country, whenever any remark, which he imagines to be slightly uncomplimentary, is made. Probably his comprehension of what has been said is exceedingly incomplete, but he labours under the idea that the " Vaterland " has been slightingly spoken of, and he accordingly demands an apology, and, if very young and of the student class, burns to add another to the array of scars with which his face is disfigured. He only gets laughed at, however, by our countrymen, and I have often wondered what would be the result if an Englishman, skilled in boxing, proposed

to settle the dispute with his fists.   But it is pleasant
to bear in mind the very charming specimens of
the German nation whom most of us, who have
travelled much, must have met   No one can have
ever failed to enjoy the society of the cultivated and
intelligent Germans, who whilst speaking several
languages, unlike their less courteous countrymen,
never correct or appear to notice the mistakes of
the foreigner who tries to talk to them in their own
tongue. Germans are most persevering in their
attempts to speak English, and they generally
accept, with much good nature, the involuntary
smiles which some of their remarks cause.

Some years ago a German, who had been sent to
Davos for the winter, was asked why his doctor had
recommended the place to him. He much as-
tonished his questioner by replying, " I was sent
here for blood-shedding." In other words, he was
a hæmorrhage patient.

A German friend, wishing to convey to us the
information that some one in the village kept hens,
remarked, " She has the little chickens which make
eyes," and added, " I have by me always a basket
of eyes." [1]

[1] German, Ei (egg), pronounced eye.

On another occasion our friend was telling us some of his troubles, and it required all the self-control, of which we were capable, to refrain from smiling when he announced, in tones of much distress, "I have lost five parents,[2] and my father mourned greatly."

One day I was shopping at St. Moritz Bad, and, on my observing to the woman at the Grand Bazaar, who was serving me, that I supposed her shop was closed in winter, she replied, "Oh, yes ; in winter we always live upstairs." This answer seemed to me somewhat irrelevant, but, when she went on to tell me that she would soon open her shop up in the village, I understood that " upstairs " meant St. Moritz Dorf.

"I do not like Miss T., she keeps always her nose upstairs," said my German friend to me one day. A *nez retroussé* was evidently a feature he did not admire.

Those who have spent several months in any of the winter Swiss health-resorts, such as St. Moritz, Davos, Maloya, Wiesen, Andermatt, or Montreux, will at once think of two officials, usually to be

[2] French, parents (relations).

met with in such places, and often forming a centre
for contending factions and cliques. I refer to the
medical and spiritual advisers. The medical ad-
viser is often a person of weak lungs, who cannot
reside in his own country, or he is an individual
whose stock of medical knowledge is not large
enough to bear distribution over anything but a very
limited colony, in this case he will probably not have
passed the Swiss examination, which is necessary
in order that he may have the right to practise.
He therefore merely exists on sufferance, having
obtained the permission of the local doctors to
practise for so long as they see fit. The answers
at the Swiss examination must be given in French
or German, an interpreter not being allowed ; but
it is said that the failures cannot generally be
attributed to a want of knowledge of either of these
languages. Possibly the examination is in itself
very difficult. The doctor may perhaps be a young
Swiss, working his way to fame, in which case
his residence will probably be short.

As he usually lives in the same hotel as his
patients, his influence over them is very great, and
it is by his advice that they go in spring to the

lakes of Geneva and Lucerne, or to Thusis, Ragaz,
Seewis, or Promontognio.

I must utter a protest against the very unwise
habit, which is not unfrequent, of medical men
sending their patients to places, which they have not
themselves visited. They judge these places merely
from their altitude above sea-level, and from their
position with regard to the neighbouring mountains;
these facts being mostly gathered from an examination of the map, from the pages of a guide-book,
or, worse still, from the ignorant chatter of irresponsible persons, who are only too ready, after a
stay of twenty-four hours in a place, to give their
opinion upon its climate, and to advise their friends
to go there or not to go there, as the case may be.
These people, of course, know nothing of the wants
of delicate invalids, of the peculiarities of the climate,
regarding the Bise, Föhn, and other winds, during
certain months of the year, and, possibly, though
they may be aware that an English chaplain re-
sides in the hotel, they can't remember whether
there is a doctor within one or ten miles' distance.
I have heard of people being sent to Soglio in early
spring, where but few of the rooms had stoves, to

Chateau d'Oeux, where the accommodation was miserable and the food atrocious ; to Alvenau Bad when the hotel was still closed and the doctor away ; and to other places, against which there were quite as many objections. Therefore I would impress on delicate people, as strongly as I can, not to consent to start on a wild-goose chase, half across Switzerland, without, first of all, having a sound opinion from some disinterested person as to the suitability of the health resort for which they are bound.

It is, I know, a very sweeping thing to say, but I may state, after much thought, that I shall be surprised to know of any place so suitable for delicate persons in the month of April, when the winds in the heights are keen and the air in the plains is damp, as Seewis, above the Prättigau. I am aware that patients may hear that the food is bad there. This assertion I must answer, in order to save time and spare hotel-keepers' feelings by unpleasant comparisons in order to get a standard to go by, simply with a flat contradiction. What Seewis may have been I know not. Of what it is, I can speak from my own experience. I have tried Thusis,

Les Avants, Glion, Montreux, Chamonix, Meran, Wiesen, Davos, and other places in the month of April, and Seewis is by far the most suitable, owing to its extremely sheltered situation, its position on a steep slope 1200 feet above the Prattigau, and 3300 feet above the sea, and the shady walks amongst the orchards, in which the lovely little village is smothered. Seewis is reached in two hours' drive from Landquart, the road turning off at Pardisla from that which continues to Davos. The scenery is beautiful, and walks and excursions, suitable for those who can only saunter along, for a few minutes at a time, on flat ground, and for the robust, who will think nothing of the seven hours' ascent of the Seesaplana, can be had in all directions. Herr Hitz, of the Kurhaus, is a very civil and attentive host.

WIESEN.

CHAPTER III.

THE DIAVOLEZZA IN WINTER WITHOUT GUIDES.

Morbid interest displayed by many people in accidents which have terminated fatally—Works of Mr. Whymper and Dr. Emile Zsigmondy—The danger of small excursions undertaken without sufficient precautions—We set out for the Diavolezza—Bad snow—Mr. S. suffers greatly from fatigue—The Pers glacier—Darkness overtakes us—Mr. S. leads us through the séracs—Tracks at last—A mauvais pas—We lose sight of the tracks and Mr. S. feels very faint—He is almost unable to walk—Two anxious hours—The foot of the glacier is reached—We meet a relief-party at Pontresina.

THE morbid interest which many people take, in reading the details of fatal accidents, is especially noticeable if we mention Mr. Whymper's charming book, "The Ascent of the Matterhorn," to any reader of that work, outside the circle of climbers.

The first remark usually made is, "What a dreadful accident that was in which poor Lord Francis Douglas was killed! How wonderful the

description of it is!" Then comes the old thread-
bare observations about the rope, followed by "Mr.
Whymper had a marvellous escape when he tumbled,
head foremost, down that place which there is such
a striking picture of!" The illustration of two
climbers ascending some rocks, and the third shooting down over the heads of the others, in Dr. Emile
Zsigmondy's "Les dangers des Montaignes," should
make the fortune of that work, amongst a certain
class, did not the pathetic circumstances under
which it was published, give it, in any case, a place
which is unique amongst books on climbing.

I have nothing tragic to offer to my readers, yet
some of my walks have all but had fatal termina-
tions, so, perhaps, the recital of a few of them may
not be quite devoid of interest. On easy passes
and humble mountains the greatest risks have
been run by me, and, while ascending such peaks
as the Weisshorn or Dent du Géant with safety,
I have nearly come to grief on Piz Julier, the Col
du Tour, and, deepest degradation of all, the
Stelvio!

Let me first relate the particulars of a most uncomfortable day spent on the Diavolezza.

A year or two ago, I found myself at Pontresina.
It was winter, and the ugly moraine of the
Morteratsch Glacier, as well as its gaping crevasses,
were deeply buried in snow. Any one walking over
the treacherous surface had but to step on one of
the yielding snow bridges, and the slender support
breaking away under the weight, he might easily
have been precipitated to unknown depths. Therefore the danger to a single traveller was great,
but, if several persons were together, they could
use a rope and thus check the fall of any one of
them and walk in safety on the glacier.

I had crossed the pretty little Diavolezza pass
in summer, and, consequently, the way was familiar
to me. Some friends then staying at St. Moritz
were anxious to make the excursion with me, and
I very stupidly volunteered to accompany them as
guide. My companions were both apparently
strong men, one of them being the German who
had ascended the Julier with me, and the other an
Englishman, whom we will call Mr. S. We started
one cloudless morning, and, driving as far as the
Bernina Houses, left our conveyance there, and,
loading ourselves with rope, knapsacks, and ice

axes, began to ascend the deeply-covered slopes of
snow.

Mr. S. soon found the walk very tiring, in
spite of the order of our progress, in which he
came last. The snow was nearly to our knees, and,
after a time, we gratefully welcomed some rocks,
which enabled us to mount with less fatigue. We
advanced very slowly. Mr. S. had often to stop
and rest, and it was a quarter past two o'clock by
the time we reached the summit of the pass. I
feared that Mr. S. was too tired to undertake the
long walk on the other side, so I urged our return
to the Bernina Houses. This would have been a
matter of an hour or so, as the tracks were now
made, and there were slopes down which we could
have glissaded. But after a rest, Mr. S. felt himself again, and, his pluck overcoming his discretion,
he insisted on our continuing our route as we had
originally intended.

A short and steep descent brought us to the
level of the Pers Glacier, which, at this point, must
be crossed to a rock, between it and the Morteratsch
Glacier, called the Isla Pers. We tied ourselves
together, and I took the lead, Mr. S. came next,
and Mr. H. was last on the rope. The snow was

extremely soft, and, at every step, I carefully
sounded with my axe, sometimes uncovering
ghastly looking chasms, into the blue depths of
which one peered without seeing the bottom.
Great caution was necessary, and we had to zigzag
in order to cross the crevasses transversely, as,
otherwise, the whole party might have broken into
one at the same time. At last we scrambled on to
the rocks of Isla Pers. It was beginning to get
dusk, and, by the time we had glissaded to the
level of the Morteratsch Glacier, the light had
almost failed. I was much annoyed with myself
for being unprovided with a lantern, an omission
which had, once before, obliged me to spend a night
on the snow, at a height of 11,000 feet on the
Grandes Jorasses. But regrets were useless. We
hurried on. Twenty minutes brought us to the
séracs, child's play in summer, but most formidable under the conditions in which we found them.
I may here explain that séracs are pinnacles of
ice, generally separated from each other by profound crevasses. As I paused an instant to try and
discover the best place for forcing a way through
them, Mr. S. asked,—

"Do you know this part of the glacier well?"

"No," I replied, "I have been here once before in summer, and I walked with you and Mr. H., a few days ago, for a little distance amongst the séracs."

"Then may I lead, as I have often been as far as this?" inquired Mr. S.

I answered that I should be delighted if he would try and get us out of the labyrinth in which we found ourselves.

I undid the rope and tied myself in Mr. S.'s loop, and, giving the cord a twist round my axe, we started.

Soon Mr. S. called "Hold tight here! we are near the Grand Moulin!"[1] I planted my axe deeply in the snow, and let out the rope, inch by inch, while our leader felt his way cautiously down a steep slope.

"All right! we have passed it! you can come!" he cried presently, and I advanced, held in my turn by Mr. H. To my right, about three feet

[1] A moulin, or glacier mill, is a shaft in the ice, hollowed out by falling water. An unroped person, falling into a moulin, would be almost certain to lose his life, and, even if he were roped, it would require much strength to pull him up, the walls of the moulin being so smoothly polished.

from me, I could just discern, through the gloom, a large gaping hole, in which, far down, water gurgled. We had been on the look-out for this moulin for some time, and were glad to have found it. We were now sure that we were walking in the right direction. An hour passed, and then Mr. S. stopped. "This is becoming serious," he said, "we don't seem to be advancing at all, and I feel my strength failing me." It had indeed been weary work both for mind and body, and great was my relief, on stooping down to examine something which had attracted my attention, to find that it was a line of tracks running parallel to our route.

"Look!" I exclaimed, "here are tracks! our tracks of four days ago when we picnicked on the glacier! We are all right now."

Alas! We little knew that, in an hour or so, a more serious danger than any we had encountered that day would have to be faced!

But first there was a *mauvais pas* to be got over, which had given us some trouble even in daylight. It consisted in a narrow ridge of ice, which ran for ten or twelve feet, between deep crevasses. At its termination a jump had to be made over a wide

E

chasm. We were now approaching this ridge
and anxiously looking out for it. At last we
reached it, and, sitting down, I paid out the rope to
Mr. S., whose axe at once fell to work in the construction of some new steps, our footholds of a few
days before having melted away. The other end of
the ridge was a mere knife-edge, and, as he neared
it, I had to support him as well as I could with the
rope, for it was not easy for him to preserve his
balance while he worked. After twenty minutes or
so he called, "Advance close to me and give me all
the rope you can, I must jump." I joined him, let
out all the rope possible and off he went in the
darkness, coming down with a heavy thud on the
other side of the crevasse. Mr. H. then advanced
to my side, and, on hearing Mr. S.'s cheering remark,
"There's plenty of room over here!" I sprang
with all my strength in the direction in which Mr.
S. had taken his departure and came down, buried
nearly up to my neck in soft snow. Then Mr. H.
performed an acrobatic feat resembling ours, and
we felt that the rest of our route would be plain
sailing, a delusion from which we were destined
speedily to recover.

After walking for about ten minutes, it seemed to me that we were bearing too much to the right. "Are you sure that this is the right way," I inquired.

"Well, no," replied Mr. S., "the fact is I am so tired that I feel quite stupid."

I went up to him, and, in truth, he seemed far from well. Some brandy from Mr. H.'s flask revived him a little, and then we changed places and I took the lead. First I returned for a short distance in our tracks, then bore away to the left. Our old footmarks were evidently obliterated, for we lost sight of them soon after emerging from the séracs.

After a little time, Mr. S.'s strength again forsook him, and he sat down on a stone, saying that he felt very faint. The remains of the brandy did him good, but there was still a long distance to be traversed, before we could hope to be clear of the glacier.

I hastily reviewed the situation in my mind. If our poor friend were to faint, Mr. H. would have to remain with him while I went for help. If I accomplished my walk down the snow-covered glacier without falling into a crevasse, and reached Pontresina alive, it would still be six hours at least

before a relief-party could join those left on the
glacier, and, by that time Mr. S. might be frozen,
owing to his helpless condition and inability to
keep himself warm with exercise. One thing only
could be done for the time being. We placed
ourselves on either side of Mr. S., giving him our
arms. Then, carefully prodding the snow at every
step, we slowly advanced. I need not dwell on
our frequent halts, and our great fear lest Mr. S.
should fall in a faint on the snow ; but it will easily
be understood how terribly anxious we were during
the next two hours, till, finally, we realized that the
danger was over and the end of the glacier all but
reached.

It was 11 p.m., when, at length, we cast ourselves
on the snow, and rested our weary limbs in one good
slide, which landed us amongst the stones at the
foot of the glacier. We made the best of our way
towards the restaurant, and were overjoyed to see a
light, shining through the trees beyond the little
inn. It turned out to be the lamp of a conveyance
sent from Pontresina to wait for us.

As we drove into the village, lanterns could be
seen flitting to and fro, and, emerging from the door

of the Krone, was Hans Grass, followed by several
other guides, who were laden with coils of rope,
shovels, provisions, and other necessaries for our
rescue. Very hospitable did the shelter of the
hotel seem, after our prolonged excursion, and warm
was the welcome which we received from our friends,
who had been very anxious about us, and who still
believed that we risked our necks on that occasion,
in spite of the naïve remark, with which Mr. H.
attempted to reassure them that "there was no
danger, all the crevasses were covered with snow!"

CHAPTER IV.

THE STELVIO UNDER SNOW.

Our plans for the Ortler district—We start for Santa Catarina—A fair porter—The hotel is closed—Our porter conducts us to a small inn of uninviting appearance—Cupelin's three pieces of information—We are driven back to Bormio by bad weather—We decide to reach Tyrol by the Stelvio—We take a carriage and are joined by two Germans who are going our way—Cupelin's treasures—The fourth cantonière—The carriage can go no further—Difficulty in procuring porters —We speak our mind—At last we get under weigh— Our German companions—I am forced to make the tracks—My maid faints, and my hands are frost-bitten —Preparations for spending the night on the Stelvio— A primitive lodging—Cupelin cuts up the staircase for firewood.

I WAS staying at Bormio, in northern Italy, and wished to do a little climbing in the Ortler group before going to Meran. It was late in autumn, and the snow had already crept down the hills and approached the valleys. My guide, Edouard Cupelin, of Chamonix, joined me at the Bagni Nuovi at Bormio, and our plans were as follows. He and I were to go to Santa Maria, and to sleep there, and, meeting a guide previously ordered from Sulden, to cross a pass with him into the Suldenthal. On arriving there, we intended to ascend the Ortler, and as many of the other peaks in that district as the weather would give us time for. Meanwhile, both maid and luggage were to cross the Stelvio in the diligence and join me at Sulden.

The weather was unsettled, not bad enough to lead us to think that it would not be fine next day, and not fine enough to make our minds easy as to the result of a start. However, we had often set out for excursions in worse weather, and found it improve afterwards, so we decided to start for Santa Catarina on the day after my guide's arrival.

The afternoon following that on which Cupelin joined me we took a carriage, and provided ourselves with a cold turkey, a tin of soup, some potted meat, a bottle of Marsala, and one of chapagne. We were thus to a certain extent independent of the resources of Santa Catarina, and the quantity and quality of our provisions is noteworthy, as they afterwards played a leading part in the performance, into the details of which I shall presently enter.

Half an hour after quitting the town of Bormio, the road suddenly came to an end. A large slice of it had been washed down by the recent rains, and it was quite impossible for the carriage to advance any further.

"We must find a porter, and walk," observed my guide. The driver looked about, and, at length, hailed a girl who was coming up the valley, with an empty basket on her back. She was young, and slight, and pretty, and I was much surprised at the immense weight she carried without the least apparent effort. All the provisions and my knap-sack, were placed in her basket, and she insisted on taking the rope also. When she began to walk she went so quickly that we were obliged to beg her to go slower. When I say "beg," I refer to the various signs which we made to convey our

wishes to her, for she spoke only Italian, and we
did not understand a word of that language. On
arriving at Santa Catarina, we found, as we had
feared would be the case, that the hotel was already
closed, so we proceeded to hunt for a lodging in
the village. We twisted our faces and our hands
into many contortions, indicative of our wants, and
Cupelin assailed our porteress with a torrent of
Chamonix *patois*. She seemed to understand what
we were looking for and signed to us to follow her.
After a short time she stopped before a grimy-
looking cottage, and called. At the sound a
number of chickens emerged from the door, then
a pig, and finally the landlady, for this was an inn!
She nodded with a cheering air of comprehension, when Cupelin dangled first a knapsack and
then a rope and axe, before her eyes, typical of a
night's lodging and departure on the morrow across
the mountains. We followed her across the street
to what looked like a loft, but was, in reality, the
dépendance of the hotel.

The room assigned to me was far superior to
what I had dared to hope for, so I installed myself,
and sent out Cupelin to explore, and see if he

could find the guide from Sulden. In an hour
he returned with three pieces of information. First,
that the man from Sulden had not arrived, but
that another guide could be obtained, if required.
Secondly, that the weather was as bad as it could
possibly be; and thirdly, that there was not a
single soul in the village who could speak any
language excepting Italian. He said that he had
given vent to his ideas freely in his native *patois*
with admirable effect.

Next morning, at 5 a.m., Cupelin knocked at
my door, saying that the rain continued to fall
steadily, and that, whenever the mist lifted, the
hills could be seen heavily covered with fresh
snow. Clearly there was no chance of our being
able to cross to Sulden that day, and it seemed
very probable that the weather on the day following would be just as bad. A stay at Santa Catarina at that time of year, and in a dense fog, did
not possess many charms, and, as even the amusement of sitting in a room which was *salle à manger*,
kitchen, and poultry-yard all in one, might pall
after a time, we determined to tear ourselves away
from our luxurious surroundings and return to

Bormio. Packing up the remains of our provisions and our other possessions, we started for our muddy walk down the valley through the drizzling rain.

Arrived at Bormio, we discussed the advisability of remaining there till the weather should improve, or of going over the Stelvio at once to Meran, and hoping for better things in Tyrol. A decided brightening of the heavens made us finally decide on the latter course, and then, having settled that we were to cross the Stelvio, the question arose as to how it was to be accomplished. The diligence had ceased to run for a week or more, though, till then, this piece of information had not leaked out, and vague rumours were current that there were five feet of snow on the summit of this, the highest pass in Europe crossed by a carriage-road. However, the landlord promised to give us a carriage, which he thought would be able to reach the top of the pass, and, once there, we could walk down the other side. Had Cupelin and I been alone, we should have done the whole journey on foot, but the maid and luggage had to be considered, and it was inconvenient to send them by the long round

via Colico, Como, Milan, and Verona, the diligences,
which take the shorter route, having all stopped
running, owing to the fearful state of the roads, in
consequence of the heavy rains. I gave my maid
the choice of accompanying me over the Stelvio or
going round, and as she much preferred the former,
and was strong, I had no hesitation in allowing
her to do as she wished.

I therefore sent all the luggage by *grande
vitesse*, *via* Milan, except two small portmanteaus,
which a couple of porters would be able to carry
for us from the pass to Trafoi, and at Trafoi,
another carriage could be had. Our plans stood
thus when the dinner-bell rang.

There were two Germans dining at *table d'hôte*,
the only visitors remaining in the hotel. They
had been waiting for some time to cross the Stelvio,
so I suggested that we should all travel over
together, as a strong party would be an advantage.
The landlord engaged to supply us with a comfortable carriage, drawn by four horses, and the
driver was to have orders to go as far as ever he
could. Cupelin had carefully treasured up the
wine and tinned meat, and he also foraged in our

rooms for candle-ends, which were articles to which he attached much value. Cupelin's habit of hoarding up what, at the time, often seemed useless rubbish, frequently stood us in good stead, but seldom more so than during the next twenty-four hours.

The morning broke grey and cloudy, but the rain had ceased to fall, and as we slowly crawled up the long windings of the road, we speculated how soon the bleak, brown slopes would give place to snow. The road began to be covered with a thin sprinkling, soon after reaching the second Cantonierè. On arriving at the third, the snow began to ball a good deal on the wheels, and the driver had often to get down and knock it off. A short distance below the fourth Cantonierè (which is the Italian Custom-house), it became impossible for the vehicle to advance any further, so we alighted and trudged through the deep, soft snow, till we reached the very dirty and primitive inn. The driver and Cupelin brought the luggage and then returned for the horses. When we had ordered something to eat, we inquired for porters to carry our luggage over the pass to Trafoi. One and all, they refused point-blank, in spite of the

eloquence of one of the Germans, who was the
only member of the party able to speak to them in
Italian.   He asked them their reasons for declining
to accompany us.   They replied that they were
afraid of avalanches.   He then inquired if they
would go, at least, to the summit of the pass, for it
occurred to us that we could leave the luggage
at a little deserted road-mender's house there, and
the next day two men from Trafoi might be sent
up to fetch it.   We also had an idea that the Italian
porters might be willing to go so far as long as
they were not obliged to cross the frontier, unpleasant results sometimes ensuing to persons
doing so, whose ideas about free trade do not quite
correspond with the law of the land.   The porters
assured us that they feared avalanches on the
Italian side of the pass also.   The slope being but
little steeper than that from Hyde Park Corner to
Hyde Park Gate, this excuse was obviously absurd,
so I asked our German friend, who did not know
the road, to inform the men that I had crossed the
Stelvio twice during the past month, and consequently knew the pass well enough utterly to dis-
believe such statements as to avalanches on the

Italian side, and that I feared they were either excessively lazy or utter cowards. These strong remarks, aided by some uncomplimentary observations from Cupelin, delivered in Chamonix *patois*, had the desired effect, and the men consented to carry our luggage to the summit of the pass, the innkeeper looking very sulky because we should thus escape the inhospitable shelter of his roof, under which he had fully decided that we should spend the night.

The afternoon was advancing, so we got under weigh as quickly as possible. The snow was certainly very, very bad ; in fact Cupelin and I secretly agreed that we had never seen it worse, but we made light of it before our faint-hearted porters.

One of the Germans was fat and portly. He puffed like a grampus, and continually got into drifts and holes up to his waist. He then scrambled out as best he could, and continued any remark he might have been making at the moment of his exit, his observations being usually most cheerful ones, for he evidently considered the whole thing a very good joke. His companion was thin and small, and appeared fully aware of all the discomforts of the situation, which were, in his case, greatly exaggerated by the thin elastic-sided boots which he wore. My maid trudged along pluckily at the end of the procession, while Cupelin, a heavy knapsack on his back, hovered about and encouraged every one by turns. One of the Italians headed the troop, but, after a little time, he halted, and proceeded to inform me in very bad French that he contemplated returning home. I replied in the sternest and most scornful tones which I could assume, that perhaps, if I made the tracks, he might manage to walk in them. I hoped that this would spur him on and induce him to exert himself, but he merely stood aside, in order to let me pass to the front, and looked as if, on the whole, he considered that I had taken a mean advantage of him.

Cupelin, in the meantime, was a long way behind, engaged in a war of words with the other porter, who also wished to back out of his engagement. For an hour or so I pushed steadily forward, ploughing through powdery snow, which often reached to my waist. Then the Italian offered to change places with me for a little, and so, working slowly onwards, we at length reached the

stone pillar which marks the frontier between Italy
and Austria.[1] Snow was falling, and a strong wind
howled round us, and all distant objects were obscured by the driving mist. None of the other
members of the party were, as yet, in sight, so I
spent the time while waiting for them in con-
templating the not very lively prospect of the
descent, which we were soon to make, of the slopes
just below. By keeping as much as possible out
of the gullies, and descending, one above the other,
in as straight a line as we could, it seemed to me
that we should avoid all risk from avalanches.
Still the idea of the long distance which lay between
us and Trafoi, and the fact that it was already
beginning to get dusk, failed to give me any grati-
fication.

Glancing back down the long furrow which we
had made through the snow, a tall figure with a
bundle on its back could be seen, and, presently,
two more individuals also came into sight. I tried
to make out my maid amongst them, but failed to
identify her, and, as the party approached, I was
much puzzled by her absence. When, however,

[1] The Stelvio is 9000 feet above the level of the sea.

F

they nearly reached us, I noticed that, at every step, Cupelin sank nearly twice as deeply into the snow as we had done, and that he appeared to be in an unaccountable state of intense heat and fatigue. As soon as he got quite close to us, the mystery was suddenly solved, for, on his back, fastened with shawls, and her face as white as the snow itself, was my maid, in a state of complete unconsciousness. I was horrified, fearing that the case was very serious, but Cupelin reassured me saying that he felt sure she had fainted, owing to being in a much higher air than she was accustomed to, and that now he was able to apply restoratives she would speedily recover. He told me that he had carried her on his back, without once halting, for an hour. Placing my maid for a moment on the luggage, he went over to the road-mender's house. A blow or two from his powerful axe sent in the door with a crash. A ladder led upstairs to a loft, and, up this ladder, Cupelin transported my maid, asking me to fetch his flask as quickly as I could. I had taken off my gloves in order to rub my maid's hands, and, not waiting to put them on again, I ran as fast as I could to where the luggage had been left, a little distance from the house. In my hurry I tripped and fell once or twice, and consequently made my hands terribly cold as I plunged them in the snow to aid myself to get up again. By the time I reached our baggage, I no longer had any sensation left in my fingers, and could only put my arm through a strap attached to my knapsack and pull it along, and, no one being in sight, I was unable to ask for help. My return was therefore rather a slow process, and, in spite of my endeavours to bring back sensation into my hands, by rubbing them with snow, I utterly failed. By the time I entered the house, both my hands were perfectly white and dead. It was a decided case of frost-bite. My maid was just beginning to recover from her long faint, and a little brandy brought her completely to. On noticing my hands, Cupelin instantly poured out some cognac and rubbed it over them. After a short time my arms began to ache fearfully, then I felt in my hands all those tortures of returning sensation incident to frost-bite, and, as Cupelin continued to rub, the whiteness gave place to a darker hue, and finally complete sensation returned.

The two porters, after having carried our luggage into the house, took their leave and went home, while the remaining five of us consulted as to what our next step should be. The short afternoon had nearly closed in, and the scramble down to Trafoi would have been a serious matter at that hour, even had my maid been quite well, but, after our experience of the last few hours, we felt convinced that our wisest course was to remain where we were for the night, and, early next morning, descend to Trafoi, my maid being pulled down the slopes, wrapped in a rug, should she feel unequal to walking. As soon as this decision was arrived at, we began to unpack our stores and to make ourselves as comfortable as was possible under the circumstances.

The house consisted of a sort of cellar (possibly a stable), below, and a loft, approached by a ladder, above. In this room there was a rough hearth and a chimney to carry off the smoke ; also two small windows from which the glass seemed long ago to have departed. Furniture there was none, nor was there a bundle of hay or straw ; the place was as bare as it possibly could be. The operation of

making ourselves comfortable was carried out in
this wise. First of all, Cupelin brought up the door
which he had broken in. It was placed across the
two portmanteaus, thus forming a table. A candle,
which Cupelin triumphantly produced from the
depths of one of his pockets, was lit and made to
stand upright on the table. With a few sticks,
which the porters had dug up from under the
snow, a fire was kindled, and soon our eyes were
smarting in a manner which must be expected if
a fire is lit under a chimney which is half blocked
up with snow. My maid, being the invalid of the
party, was placed in the most sheltered corner,
and an impromptu couch made for her with
our wraps. Then we cooked the dinner. The
soup was heated, mixed with snow, in a large
tin, from which we first removed a potted
tongue; and on our tinned soup, potted meat,
champagne and marsala, did we feast The
German, who was of a lively turn of mind, made us
a speech, in which he lauded what he was pleased
to call our courage, and made the best of everything, while his friend, who was less cheerfully
inclined, contemplated his shrivelled boots, and

looked as if he were pondering on the stock of rheumatism he was laying up. *Table d'hôte* concluded, we all tried to get a little sleep. Cupelin did the best he could for us. The two Germans had an ulster of mine between them to protect them against a temperature many degrees below freezing-point. I had the rope as my pillow and a thin shawl as my sole wrap, and when he had settled us, Cupelin took some stones, which he had put in the fire to heat, and placed them against our feet. He himself would not lie down, but sat over the crackling wood, carefully gathering the little bits together from time to time, and thus economizing our limited stock of fuel. The weary hours passed terribly slowly; sleep under such conditions of discomfort was quite impossible, and as the fire gradually died out the cold became intense. My gloves, lying near me, grew hard as steel, and at last I could bear it no longer, so softly rose and went over to where Cupelin was sitting.

"Cupelin," I whispered, "it is intensely cold; have we *no* more wood?"

"None, madam," he replied; and adding somewhat inconsistently, as it seemed to me, " But I shall soon get some," he left the room.

Immediately after heavy blows were heard outside.

" What is that ? " cried both the Germans at once.

" I don't know," I answered ; " I'm just going to see." As I spoke Cupelin entered, carrying several large pieces of wood.

" Where did you succeed in finding all that wood ? " I inquired in surprise.

" Oh, it's part of the stairs," replied my guide, as he heaped up some of it on the hearth. "The staircase is the only wooden thing in the house, except the door ; we will send a few francs from Trafoi in payment."

This fresh supply of wood kept us tolerably warm until the morning broke, grey and cloudy as the day before. But this chapter is passing beyond all reasonable limits, so I will keep the account of what happened to us, when we said good-bye to the road-mender's house, for the next.

CHAPTER V.

THE FLOODS OF 1882 IN AUSTRIA AND NORTHERN ITALY.

Return of the porters—We are persuaded to go back to the
Custom-House—The officials speed the parting guests—
We go down to the Muster Thal by the Wormser Joch
—Arrival at Mals—We hear about the floods—The
Germans leave us—State of the road to Meran—We
reach Meran—We plan a small excursion—A porter is
engaged who suffers from continual hunger—He accepts
our offer to remain till our return at the foot of the peak
—He shows us our destination—We find that the point
indicated is not the summit—A long *détour*—We give
chase to the porter who has not waited for us—His sack
is found to be empty—The porter still suffers from
hunger—Cupelin starts for Chamonix and I set out for
Montreux—The floods—The manner in which wood is
collected at Meran—Trent—Appearance of Verona after
the inundation—We reach Switzerland.

WHEN the light grew strong enough for us to
begin our packing, we set to work and made our
preparations for going down to Trafoi. All that

we should require till the next day was put into Cupelin's knapsack, the rest of the goods were packed in the portmanteaus, which we should have to leave on the pass, till some porters from Trafoi could be sent up to fetch them.

Breakfast was, of course, out of the question, as nothing remained from our slender stock of provisions. We hoped that a couple of hours would enable us to reach Trafoi, which uncomfortable little place seemed to us, in the dim and distant future, even as the flesh-pots of Egypt. Just as Cupelin was engaged in uncoiling the rope, in order to fasten my maid up in a rug with it, loud shouts were heard outside, and tramping up through the snow we saw our two porters of the day before, accompanied by two custom-house officers. We triumphed much at the sight, for we imagined that it meant repentance on the part of the porters ; but, alas ! their motive, when it was disclosed, did not consist in an offer to carry our luggage to Trafoi. The party conducted their manœuvres with tact, however. First, opening one of their knapsacks, they produced coffee and bread, inquiring, with apparent interest, how we felt. Then one of the

custom-house officials disclosed the real object of
this early visit. He said that it was expressly
forbidden for any one to cross the Stelvio once
the snow is down, and that should we, in breaking
this rule, meet with an accident, the custom-house
authorities would be blamed for allowing us to
pass and he might, in consequence, lose his place.
He promised, if we would return to the custom-
house with him, to supply us with porters, who
would carry our luggage to Santa Maria in the
Musterthal, whence we could get a carriage, and
reach Meran next day. He would also pro-
vide us with a hand-sledge, on which my maid
could be pulled for a good part of the distance.
Such an offer was not to be despised, so we turned
our backs on the inhospitable building in which we
had spent the night, and were not long in reaching
the fourth Cantonière. While we had a combined
breakfast and luncheon there, the hand-sledge was
prepared and the luggage fastened on it, and, when
we came out, we found that all the men of the establishment intended to accompany us as far as the
Swiss frontier. My maid was placed on the portmanteaus, and tied to them by the aid of shawls

and the rope, and off we started. A camera would have been very welcome at that moment, for a funnier procession I never saw.

Cupelin and I were in front, closely followed by the stout German, who got himself into holes as usual, and with his habitual cheerfulness remarked, as he emerged on all fours, " C'est comme (gasp) le Boulevard des Italiens ! " Then came the sledge, with my maid perched high up on the luggage. Two strong porters made light of the weight, and a custom-house officer walked on each side, steady-ing the sledge, and giving encouragement in a, to her, unknown tongue. Some nondescript persons straggled along behind, and a small yellow dog, who continually disappeared in the snow, his ears and tail alone visible, brought up the rear. It was very pleasant when the snow gradually gave place to stones and grass, and the sight of a green forest below us, lit by the sun, which had at length con-trived to emerge from its covering of clouds, was most refreshing to our eyes, wearied as they were by the bleak, snowy landscape which we had had around us during the last twenty-four hours. Here some of our escort left us, only the two custom-

house officers and a couple of porters going on
with us to Santa Maria. The woods of chestnut
were beautifully fresh, the leaves shone like satin
after the rain, and the Musterthal seemed a very
paradise to us, as every step led us lower, where
the vegetation became more luxuriant. Soon a
cluster of white houses peeped through the trees,
and we arrived at the village. We feasted right
royally at the clean little inn, and then ordered a
carriage to take us to Mals. Two small vehicles
were prepared for us, and away we went, along a
narrow country road, strewn with large stones, and,
in some places, with trunks of trees. The jolting
was fearful, and even Cupelin exclaimed from time
to time that he'd never seen anything like it in his
life (an expression of opinion not uncommon
amongst guides, as Mr. Dent truly remarks[1]). On
reaching the Austrian frontier, our luggage was
mercilessly examined, and a long delay consequently ensued, so that it was dark before the lights
of Mals could be seen, twinkling through the heavy
rain, which fell during the last hour of our drive.

[1] " Above the Snow Line," by Clinton Dent. This delightful book will amuse and interest people who have never
even seen a mountain.

The hotel at Mals was cold and cheerless, but we were not disposed to be critical after our late experiences. I noticed as I entered the dining-room, that the two Germans were evidently listening to some news which did not please them, judging from the expressions of their faces, and the way in which they ejaculated the German equivalents for "fearful!" "terrible!" and "dreadful!" at intervals, whenever the landlord paused in his narrative. I was not left long in doubt as to the subject of the conversation, for, as soon as they saw me, they hastened to tell me that they were informed by the hotel-keeper that a great part of Tyrol was under water, that many of the roads and railways were completely washed away, the line in the Pusterthal being destroyed from end to end, and piles of stones which had been swept down the lateral valleys by the swollen torrents were heaped many feet high above the rails in some places. The landlord had also told them that the valley between Meran and Botzen was simply a lake, and all communication cut off between the two places, the letters and provisions coming round the other way. This necessitated a wide *détour*, and, should the road in

question be, in its turn, destroyed, the hundreds
of invalids then staying at Meran would have a
most trying time.   Many people stop there in the
autumn for a month, or so, before going to the
Riviera for the winter, and most of the visitors are
lung patients in a very delicate state of health.
These poor people could not, of course, undertake
a journey to the south, which, under these conditions, must be made partly on foot, partly in
boats, and partly by carriage, often halting at
most uncomfortable night-quarters.   Therefore the
invalids had no choice but to remain at Meran
during the whole winter, as the repairing of the
line would take some months.   Meran, under any
circumstances, was not likely to suit them during
the cold weather, and, in consequence of the floods,
the provisions took so long to reach the town that
the meat was generally far from fresh by the time
it arrived, and hardly any vegetables could be
procured.   In view of such attractions, the two
Germans preferred to avoid Meran, and go straight
to Innsbruck.

The following morning I started in a conveyance called, by a somewhat strained courtesy, the

diligence, accompanied by my maid and Cupelin.
This vehicle was bound for Meran. The road was
very bad, and, in some places, great slices had been
washed away, and only a gap remained. On
these occasions the post pulled up at the edge of
the gap, the passengers alighted, and walked across
an extemporized bridge, which had been hastily
constructed of pine-trees and boards. Another
vehicle waited on the other side, and in this the
journey was continued till we came to a place
where the road was again broken away, when the
former performance had to be repeated once more.
It was a most tedious drive to Meran under these
conditions, but, at last, towards evening, we got there.
Needless to say, our luggage, sent by Grande
Vitesse from Bormio, had not arrived, and, to make
a long story short, we saw nothing of it for six
weeks, when, by aid of many telegrams and much
intelligence on the part of the *concièrge* at the
"Continental," Milan, it reached that hotel three
hours before our arrival there, and had consequently taken more than six weeks to travel from
Bormio.

Meran looked much as usual, the floods not

being visible from the village, but, though we did not see them, we heard of little else, and it was clear that, being at Meran, we had better remain there a little time till travelling became easier, as we were in no hurry to reach Montreux, where I intended to spend the winter.

It was not of any use to keep Cupelin in so non-climbing a district, and during such non-climbing weather, so I decided to send him back by Innsbruck after we had taken one walk and seen what we could of the views near Meran. The next day being tolerably fine, we settled to go up a mountain, of which I have quite forgotten the name. We were told that some scrambling was necessary in order to reach the summit. As neither of us had the least idea of the position of this mountain, or the way to approach it, we engaged a porter who volunteered to lead us in the right direction, and, at 4 a.m. the following morning, we set out in clear weather. Our porter was lanky and hungry-looking, and eyed the load of provisions which he had placed in a common sack, and tied round his neck with a string, with longing glances. About two hours after starting he suggested that he was

hungry, so we gave him a plentiful supply of
bread and cheese, and he sat down by the side
of the path to enjoy himself. His manner of
getting up the hill consisted in making dashes
down the sides of gulleys, and mounting them
again a little further on. As this mode of pro-
gression seemed likely to waste a good deal of
time, Cupelin suggested to the youth that he should
keep strictly to his vocation of porter, and allow
us to do the guiding of the party. He was nothing
loath, the way was easily found, and, before very
long, we left the trees behind, and reached a deso-
late stony tract, on which the Austrian Alpine
Club have erected a hut. The porter observed
that it would be an excellent plan to halt here for
luncheon, but we sternly bade him continue for an
hour more, and Cupelin, for about the twentieth
time that day, gave vent to the words " Vorwärts !"
and " Schnell !" words to which he seemed to
attach more importance than to all the rest of the
German language.

A little further on the ground became steeper,
and, looking back, the porter could be seen, laboriously following us in an attitude much affected by

infants of tender years.   He plaintively informed
us that he found it very difficult to get on, as he
had no nails in his boots, and consequently required
to make use of his hands as well as his feet.   We
looked to where a thin, white, wedge-like peak shot
up towards the sky, and mentally pictured our
porter's attitudes when he reached the ridge ;
judging by the early stage at which he brought all
available means of holding on into use, he would
require to be a centipede by the time he got there,
if he intended to adhere.

"Supposing we leave him here ? " Cupelin suggested.

I asked the porter if he would prefer to wait for
us under a rock near at hand, or if he very much
wished to go on.

He replied without hesitation that he would be
delighted to remain below, and furthermore added
that he was very hungry.   We sat down and had
luncheon, and then, putting two rolls and a flask in
our pockets, placed the rest of the provisions in the
sack.   They consisted of a large piece of veal and
one of beef, half a loaf of bread, a slice of cheese,
two hard-boiled eggs, and a bottle of red wine.

Leaving the sack with the porter, and taking the rope, we began to scramble over loose stones and snow, then climbed along a narrow ridge, which led us to the point shown to us from below by the porter, and declared by him to be the summit. Miserable delusion! From our standing-point the ridge still extended upwards, the snow curling in a beautiful cornice over a bare wall of rock to our left. I did not particularly relish the idea of going along this ridge with only one guide, and Cupelin also thought it imprudent, so we descended the slopes of snow to our right till they became less steep, then traversed, and finally mounted in almost a direct line to the summit. This, however, took us the greater part of two hours, and we only remained on the top for a short time. The view was a lovely one, many chains of, to us, unknown mountains rising around in wave-like ranges.

The descent straight down the slopes was quickly accomplished, but Cupelin looked in vain towards the large rock below for our porter. On stopping for a moment to try and discover his whereabouts, we caught sight of a black dot, rapidly growing smaller in the distance. This was the porter, *en route* for Meran. We supposed that he feared an accident in consequence of our long delay, and probably intended to organize a search-party, or to take his revenge in some equally playful and irritating manner for the pace at which Cupelin had made him walk that morning. Hunger prompted us to try and overtake him as speedily as possible, as the contents of his sack had many attractions for us. We ran as fast as we could, and called loudly, and, at last, the object of our pursuit stopped, and we rejoined him.

"Now, madame," said Cupelin, "please ask him to undo the sack and get out the provisions."

I translated this to the porter, but he did not appear to relish the request, and handed over his bag with an air of sulky resignation. The moment Cupelin felt its weight a loud exclamation broke from him.

"Le coquin! Il a tout mangé!"

And it was quite true; not one atom of bread or meat, or a single drop of wine remained, and the youth stood by, lean and hungry-looking as ever.

When we had freely expressed our opinion on the absence of our dinner, Cupelin observed that the porter still, perhaps, suffered from hunger, and was equal to another meal; so, by way of testing his capacities in that direction, he offered the remains of one of our rolls, which was at once eagerly accepted, and therewith consumed. Lower down, where pine-forests gave place to vineyards, that young man again found means of satisfying the ever-present pangs of hunger, for he occupied himself in attacking the grapes with a disregard of the possible danger to himself from the guardians of the vines, which our experience of his courage during the day had not led us to expect.

The morning after our excursion, Cupelin started on his return journey to Chamonix. I remained at Meran a week or two longer, and then determined to go to Montreux.

The journey, as far as Verona, appeared likely to be a very uncomfortable one, at least so the hotel-keepers said. But I find that these good people generally show over-much anxiety for the welfare of their clients, when it is a question of their departure; so I consulted with a carriage-owner, and he took a very different view of the situation.

"Oh, yes," he said, "the journey can easily be

made and won't be very long ; but the roads are
bad, and the carriage will get extremely wet, so I
cannot let you have it according to the ordinary
tariff."

This I had expected, and was very glad to have
found means of leaving the place without more
difficulty.

We started early in the morning from Meran,
and all went well till we approached Botzen. Then
we had to go through a regular lake, the water reaching half-way up the carriage-wheels. The horses
were rested for a short time at Botzen, and from there
we telegraphed to the hotel at Trent, asking the
landlord to send a carriage to meet us at the nearest
station to that town to which the train could go.
From Botzen the road became even worse than it
had been from Meran. We had to sit with our feet
on the seats of the carriage, as the water filled all
the inside of it. I thought once or twice that the
vehicle would float and the horses begin to swim.
Boats of primitive construction paddled about, and,
high on the shores of the lake, we could see regular
settlements of poor people, camped out under sheets
which formed impromptu tents, who had been lite-

rally washed out of house and home. It was very, very sad to see all round one the ruin which had been caused by the floods. The water having subsided a good deal during the last fortnight, much of the land which had been covered was now exposed to view. Vineyard after vineyard could be seen, with mud clinging to the vine leaves, and the once beautiful purple fruit hanging shrivelled and spoilt. Melons floated on the water, and, high up on trees and houses, a slimy mark told to what a depth the flood had stood in the valley. At length we reached a station from which we could go by train nearly to Trent. After making the short journey by railway, we were obliged, on alighting at the station, to walk along platforms of board, laid across rushing torrents, which, swollen with the rains, had formed many unfamiliar channels for themselves. It was dark by this time, and the sight was a weird one. Men with flaming torches stood all along, and the water boiled and surged below. We had to walk for, perhaps, ten minutes before reaching the place where it was possible for carriages to meet us.

The scene reminded me of a curious sight which

may be observed on spring nights at Meran. The wood, cut in winter in the forests bordering the river for many miles above Meran, is piled up and left at the edge of the stream. As soon as the melting of the snow in spring swells the river, a number of stakes are driven into the bed near the bridge at Meran, and a barrier formed obliquely across the water. This is left open in one narrow place only, from which a swiftly-flowing current leads, between walls, to a reservoir. The work of making this barrier concluded, the various woodmen all along the river are informed, and at once begin to throw the wood into the stream, cut in blocks some three or four feet long. Down it dashes towards Meran, and, following the strongest part of the current, most of it is carried down the small channel into the reservoir, and is there landed. Some, however, float against the barrier, and other pieces become wedged between stones. In order to free these pieces and send them into the right and narrow way, a number of men place themselves at the various points, where the wood is likely to be stopped and push it off again with long poles. In order that the river may not become filled during the night with the pieces of wood which catch in this way, the work of staving them off is continued till a very late hour, sometimes, I believe, the whole night, the men working by torchlight, and often standing in several feet of water. It is a very picturesque sight to watch them from the bridge, the lights reflected from the rushing water, and flashing on the figures of the strong-looking Tyrolese peasants who are toiling below.

But we are now at Trent, and never did the always comfortable " Hôtel de Trent " seem half so comfortable as on this occasion, after emerging from the floods. We were told that communication was open to Milan, so the next day we started by train, noticing as we left the hotel the marks of the flood on the walls as high as the first floor. Before reaching Verona we had to cross a river, the railway bridge over which had been entirely destroyed. Accordingly, the performance of getting out, walking across very tottering planks and getting into a train on the other side, had to be gone through. Verona had evidently suffered terribly from the inundation. Many of the houses by the river were mere shells, and the

water still flowed above the basements. We
arrived that evening at Milan and the following
day said good-bye to Italy, and passed by the
Mont Cenis into Switzerland. Two months at
Montreux followed, and the rest of the winter was
spent at Chamonix. I have described my climbs
there in "The High Alps in Winter ; or, Mountaineering in search of Health," so will not refer
to any of those scrambles in these pages, but will
narrate in the next chapter the adventures of a day
spent the following spring on the Glacier de Tour.

CHAPTER VI.

COL DU TOUR WITHOUT GUIDES.

We decide to make the excursion of the Col du Tour,
Fenêtre de Saléna and Col de Chardonnet—Much fresh
snow above the village of Tour—An unpleasant scramble
—We gain the glacier—A thick fog and great heat—
The pass—We are in doubt as to the prudence of crossing
the Col de Chardonnet in a fog—We reluctantly make
up our minds to go back the way we came—We do not
enjoy the descent—At ten o'clock we reach Chamonix—
Condition of our faces—The guides are not sympathetic
when at last we can leave the house.

THIS excursion was undertaken in the middle of
May. The season was a late one, and snow still
lay heavily on the ground down to a height of
5000 feet. Chamonix was very empty, but an
energetic young English clergyman, in addition to
one or two other visitors, was staying at the Hôtel
d'Angleterre. My enterprising countryman was
anxious to see as much as he could of the chain of
Mont Blanc, during the week or ten days he

intended to stay at Chamonix. I, on my part,
wanted to take some good walks and get into
training for the summer season, so we combined
our forces, and, at five o'clock one morning, we
started for the Col du Tour, intending to cross it
and return to Chamonix, *viâ* the Fenêtre de Saléna
and the Col de Chardonnet, a tour which I had
made a few months previously. Our first plan
had been to ascend to the Col du Géant, but the
uncertain state of the weather decided us to go
instead to the Col du Tour.

At a quarter past six one morning, we left our
carriage at the little village of Tour. Crossing the
meadows, we at once came upon patches of snow,
and the ground was thickly sprinkled as we began
to mount the rhododendron-covered slopes which
lead up to the level part of the glacier du Tour,
above the ice-fall. A little path gives easy access
to the plateau above, but the track was hidden by
the snow, and we had such a stiff climb to reach
the top of the slope, so steep as to be almost a
precipice, that we unanimously congratulated each
other that the weather, which had been rather
cloudy when we set out, had so much improved as

to allow us to hope that we could carry out our plan of returning by the Chardonnet Col, and so avoid the descent of a place which had given us such difficulty in ascending, hampered as we were with rope and knapsacks. A long grind up a snow-covered moraine brought us to the level part of the glacier. We tied ourselves together, and keeping the rope tightly stretched, we started once more. The snow was very soft, and, as we were only a party of two, I had to prod for crevasses with great care, as it would have been difficult for my companion to pull me out had I fallen through. The weather, though it had improved since we left Chamonix, was by no means settled. For a few minutes a blue expanse of sky, with glittering domes of snow standing out against it, could be seen. Then the mists would blot out everything, and we could not distinguish objects at a greater distance than a few yards. The glare of the snow was intensified by the white mist and the heat was most trying, as there was not a breath of air moving. When, from time to time, our surroundings became distinct, I noted the direction of the Col, which is by no means easy to find from

the Glacier du Tour, as it is not seen till within
twenty minutes of reaching it. My friend began
to find the heat and glare almost unbearable, and
had often to stop and rest. The softness of the
snow made it most fatiguing, and my weight did
not enable me to make the tracks very deep, so
that he sank in my footsteps.

It was 3.15 p.m. when we reached the pass, and,
as we mounted to the little ridge on which the
stone man is built, a rush of cold air greeted us
from the other side, and, while we had luncheon
and reviewed the situation, we became thoroughly
chilled. The question was this—should we go on,
or should we return as we came. The Fenêtre de
Saléna, a narrow pass giving access to the Glacier
de Saléna, was invisible, owing to the fog. However, I knew that I could manage to find it, as it is
very close to the Col du Tour. But to reach the
Col de Chardonnet from the Fenêtre, the wide snow-
fields of the Saléna Glacier must be traversed to
the foot of the Chardonnet Pass, and the bergschrund or crevasse below the latter must be
crossed, a possible place to get over it being found.
Step-cutting might also be necessary on the steep

slope below the summit of the Col, and an hour
and a half must be allowed before one can descend
the other side and get clear of the glacier. Not a
very promising prospect to contemplate at 3.30, in
the month of May, and in a fog! Our plan of
returning had but one drawback—the descent of
the wall up which we had scrambled in the morning
and which we had found difficult. We rapidly
decided that the latter alternative was the only
one we could with prudence adopt. Packing the
remains of our provisions, we straightway launched
forth, and after numerous plunges, and, lower
down, a good glissade, we reached the beginning
of the steep rocky slope just as it grew dark. We
were tired from the heavy walking, and, in the
dusk, exaggerated the difficulties of our morning's climb, so that we were not in the pluckiest
frame of mind possible when we began slowly to
descend.

After a few minutes, it became impossible to distinguish rocks, rhododendron bushes, and precipices
from each other, and, as a blunder between the two
last might have been somewhat awkward, we again
uncoiled the rope. It had been discarded when we

quitted the glacier, but now we attached ourselves
again, and I went down to the end of my tether.
When I was firmly placed, I drew in the rope, while
my companion descended, and so, little by little,
we approached the pastures below. At length we
reached them and walked rapidly to Argentière,
where we had coffee while a carriage was being got
ready, and at 10.10 p.m. we turned into the court-
yard of the Angleterre at Chamonix. I suppose
that the account of an excursion ought to end with
the return, but the three following days were much
more memorable to me than the events of the walk
I have mentioned. I have many times had my face
badly burnt on ice and snow, but never have I
experienced such agony as resulted from my walk
to the Col du Tour. My friend suffered quite as
severely as I did, and for four days neither of us
could leave the house. The stiffening of the skin
made opening one's mouth to eat a matter in which
all ones ingenuity was required, and the pain from
the blisters with which my face was entirely covered,
prevented me from lying down even for a moment
during the second night. A sorry spectacle we pre-
sented when at last we could leave the hotel, and

I fear, from the grins of the guides, that they were not altogether sympathetic for misfortunes contracted during an excursion accomplished without their aid.

CHAPTER VII.

FIRST ASCENT OF THE BIESHORN.
(4161 metres, or 13,652 English feet.)

A few words about the peaks of the Alps which remained
unascended in 1884—Imboden gives me some unexpected information—Appearance of the Bieshorn from
the Vispthal—We examine the mountain from the Festi
—We decide to attempt its ascent—The start—A night
below the Bruneggjoch—Our peak at close quarters—
The Biesjoch—We begin the ascent of the Bieshorn—
Excitement—"It will go somehow, but I daresay you
won't like the look of it!"—The appearance of the
arête—We have a lively two hours—Imboden loses his
axe—A virgin summit—We try a short cut in descending—A miniature avalanche—Imboden suggests a novel
mode of crossing a glacier—Back on the Bruneggjoch—
We cross the Barrjoch and descend to St. Nicholas.

ON July 24th, 1885, the last great peak of the Alps
which had remained unascended, succumbed before
the determined attack of Mr. Seymour King.

This mountain, the Aiguille Blanche de Peuteret,
had cost Professor Balfour and his guide their

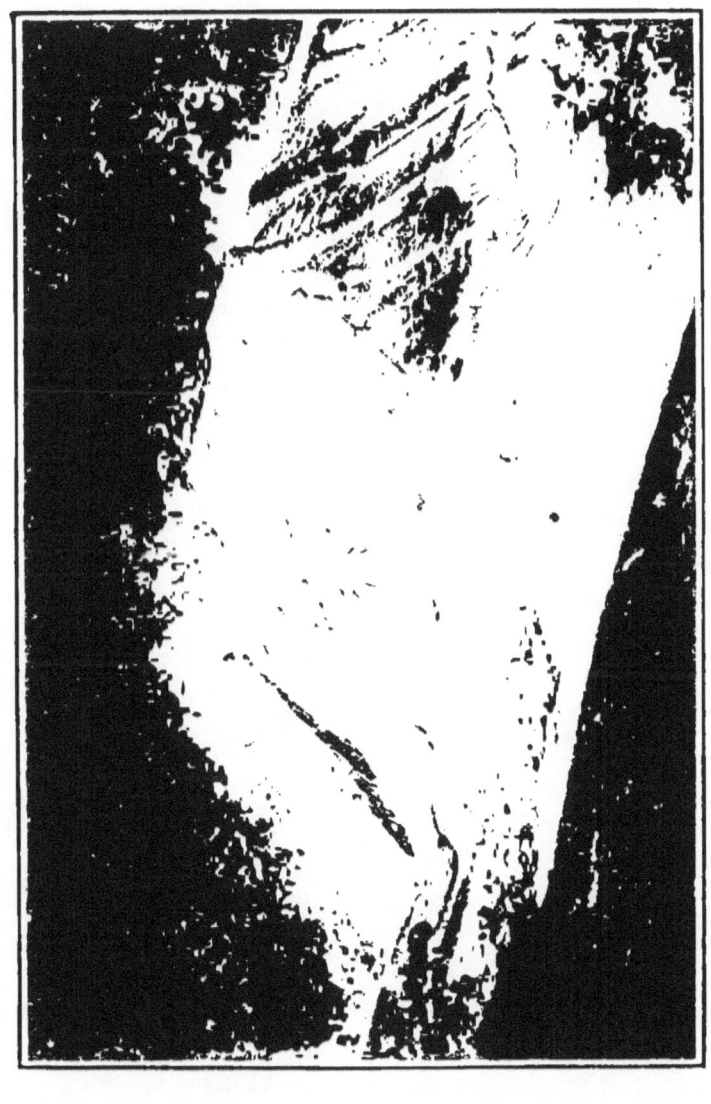

Weisshorn.   Bieshorn.

The Weisshorn and Bieshorn, from the Brunegjjoch.

Page 98.

lives in 1882, and, since that time, various un-
successful attempts had been made to ascend it,
bad weather having invariably caused those
climbers who started for the excursion to return
before advancing to any great height. I myself,
amongst others, had assaulted the mountain on
the side of the Glacier de la Brenva, and bitter
was my disappointment and that of my guides
when, after crossing the bergschrund, going for
some distance up the steep slope below the rocks,
and finding the snow excellent and the stones
too firmly frozen to bombard us, a storm came on
and we were most reluctantly obliged to retreat.
Great, therefore, was my joy, when sitting one lovely
evening in July, 1884, on the rocks of the Festi,
which is the sleeping-place for the Dom, to receive
the following information from Joseph Imboden,
my guide. He told me that for some years he had
been waiting for an opportunity to ascend one of
the two mountains which till then had not been
conquered. I was much surprised to hear that two
of the first-class peaks of the Alps remained unclimbed, while I had only known of one, and I
eagerly asked for further particulars.

"See, madame, that fine point rising to the right of the Weisshorn," he said ; " that mountain is 350 feet higher than Piz Bernina, and yet no one has ever been up it!" I looked to where he pointed and exclaimed, " But, Imboden, surely that is the Brunegghorn ! " " Madame," replied he, " ask any of the mule-drivers and second-rate guides whom you may happen to meet between Stalden and St. Nicholas, the name of the high white peak which you see while walking from one of these places to the other, and those who don't tell you that it's the Brunegghorn will assure you that it's the Weisshorn! Look far below it, *there* is the Brunegghorn."

I carefully examined the ridges, and there was no doubt of the accuracy of his statement. We at once decided to take advantage of the beautiful weather, and start for the ascent of this new peak as soon as Imboden should return from an ascent of the Matterhorn, for which he had been previously engaged. During our walk up the Dom next day, our eyes frequently wandered across the Vispthal, and we eagerly discussed the characteristics of the fine white peak opposite. Some steep rocks led to a long and narrow

ridge, plastered up with snow on the right
and falling away in steep rocky walls to the left.
We were uncertain whether it would be best for
us to follow this ridge in its entire length, or to
strike it near the summit by mounting the rocks.
The relative disadvantages of these routes were,
that, in the first case, should we find ice on the
ridge, the amount of step-cutting would be almost
prohibitory, requiring perhaps four or five hours
for the passage of the ridge alone ; and, in the
second case, the rocks were evidently, from Imboden's observation of them from the *arête* of the
Weisshorn, excessively rotten, and, as the snow
which lay on them in patches melted, we might
expect a regular bombardment by falling stones.
Hence we decided to make no definite plans till we
should be able to examine the mountain from the
Biesjoch. Of course we kept our intentions a
profound secret. Imboden had set his heart on
taking the first travellers up the peak, and had
been careful not to announce the fact of its being
unascended till he saw a reasonable probability
of carrying out his project. It seems astonishing
that so high a mountain should have hitherto

escaped notice, but its position, lying far back in the range, and only seen from the Vispthal, when it is invariably mistaken for the Brunegghorn or Weisshorn, or from the summit of the surrounding peaks, when it is passed over without notice, amongst so many other mountains, accounts for the curious fact that plans were so rarely made for its assault.

I find in Ball's "Western Alps" the following notice of the Bieshorn (as we christened it), on page 308 : "The ridge which circles round from peak 4161 " (the Bieshorn) " did not appear practicable at any point." This remark occurs in a notice of a passage of the Biesjoch, made in 1864 by Messrs. Moore, Morshead, and Gaskell, with the guides Christian Almer and Peter Perrn. Since ascending the mountain, I have met several climbers who told me that they had resolved to make the first ascent.

On the 6th August, 1884, we left Zermatt in lovely weather at ten o'clock. I was accompanied by Joseph Imboden and another guide. Our object for that day was to find a convenient nook in the rocks where we could spend the night at as high an altitude, and as near our work for the next

day, as was possible. Imboden knew all the mountain paths well, and led us up a beautiful little track
from Herbrigen, winding steeply among the rocks,
and, in three hours, bringing us to a collection of
châlets high above the last trees. Here we lounged
for a little, and admired the magnificent view of the
distant Bernese Alps, and the bold forms of the
Dom and Täschhorn, shooting up into the sky on
the other side of the valley. Then, filling some
bottles with milk, we began once more to mount.
The heat was very great, and, as the day wore on,
dark clouds gradually covered the sky, and the
thunder boomed amidst the rocks. We quickened
our pace, and, without much trouble, found a
sheltered spot under an overhanging cliff, near the
foot of the Abberg glacier.

As we lay that night in our sleeping-bags, I
noticed, with great satisfaction, that the rain
ceased and the sky slowly cleared, and when, at
2.30 a.m., we began to prepare for breakfast, all
mist had disappeared, and everything promised
well for our excursion. At 3.45 we got under
weigh and began to grope along the slippery grass
slope by the aid of our lantern. Soon we arrived

at the moraine, and then, after a little of this particularly unpleasant feature of mountain climbing,
we reached the glacier. Hastening up it, we soon
found ourselves close to the ice-fall. Now I have
a great affection for ice-falls—in their right places—
but an ice-fall in the dusk of early morning, when
one is still rather sleepy, and inclined to imagine
that the towering *séracs* above are ten times their
real size, and leaning over one at twice their actual
inclination, is not a sight to produce, at any rate,
a feeling of satisfaction. Therefore, when Imboden
asked me if I would like to go through, or pass
along the rocks, I thankfully pronounced in favour
of the latter. They required a considerable display
of gymnastics, and we were delayed for half an
hour or so by having chosen them in preference
to the snow. By 6.40 we gained the Bruneggjoch,
and from there our peak rose, white and glittering
in the sun, across the plateau of the Turtman
glacier. Imboden had a good look at it while I
took several photographs, and, as we breakfasted,
he told me that he thought our best plan would be
to go direct to the Biesjoch, and see if we could
keep along the ridge leading upwards from there.

Breakfast finished, we left the camera and one of
the bottles of wine on the Bruneggjoch, and started
off across the slopes of frozen snow towards the
Biesjoch. Thirty minutes quick walking brought
us to the bergschrund below the pass, and ten
minutes more sufficed for the step-cutting above it.
Once on the Biesjoch we had a good view of the
ridge to the right. It went up very steeply and
was fringed with snow cornices which hung over,
sometimes on one side and sometimes on the
other. The snow on the pass was loose and
powdery, and Imboden shook his head as he
noticed these unpromising details, and remarked
that it would not go. It remained, therefore,
to us to mount by the rocks, which were
already beginning to discharge their artillery of
stones down the steep snow slopes, which divided
them from the plateau of the Bies glacier. So on
we had to go with as little delay as possible, anxious
to be above those slopes before the cannonade
became still more furious. We ran down the
slope on the south side of the pass, quickly crossed
over towards the rocks, and began to ascend the
snow slope at the place which seemed the least

exposed to the falling stones. Fortunately, a good
kick from Imboden's foot always sufficed to make
our steps without waiting to cut them, and, in a
short time, we were on the rocks, from which stones
were ceaselessly pouring down on to the glacier
below, or into the bergschrund. The rocks were
excessively rotten and most irritating to climb.
Every step tended to upset stones, and, in spite of
great watchfulness, the rope was continually dis-
lodging others. An hour and a half of this sort
of work was most trying to all our tempers, and it
was a great relief to be told by Imboden, that, on
reaching a knob of rock a short distance above us,
we should, in all probability, find ourselves on
the ridge, and be able, he hoped, from that point,
to follow it to the summit. The character of this
ridge was thus the turning-point in our ascent. If
it was practicable, we should reach our goal. If it
was impracticable, the hour of the day rendered a
descent to the glacier, and an ascent from there
directly to the summit altogether out of the question,
supposing such a route to be possible. Hence it
was with great impatience that we awaited the
arrival of our leader on this knob, as on what he

might see when he reached it, depended the result
of our excursion. At length Imboden clambered
on to the rock, and, standing up, surveyed the ridge.
Then turning to us, he remarked, " It will go somehow, but I daresay you won't like the look of it."
A second or two more, and the other guide and I
emerged on to the ridge, and saw what sort of
work lay before us. We had a platform some
three or four feet square to stand on, but from
there the ridge quickly narrowed to a knife-edge
of hard snow, which, after remaining level for a
short distance, shot upwards in a narrow crest,
from which a cornice of snow curled over, and
glittering icicles hung and fell off, as they melted
in the powerful rays of the sun. I confess that
I by no means liked the look of it, and I observed to
Imboden that the ridge of the Weisshorn appeared
much less difficult. Imboden seemed amused by my
remark, and informed me that there was no com-
parison between the two, and that a person who
would not attempt to cross the ridge in front of us
might feel quite happy on the *arête* of the Weisshorn.
I ascended the Weisshorn a few weeks later, and
most thoroughly agree with him on this point.

With such enlivening conversation our appetites were sharpened for luncheon. We left all the provisions, except one bottle of wine, at the beginning of the ridge, and the heat was so great that all wraps, even our gloves, could safely be deposited there also. At 9.45 we began our long climb along the crest. The total absence of wind was greatly in our favour and enabled us to maintain our equilibrium along the first part of the ridge without difficulty. It is very impressive to look down from such an *arête*, and it is rarely that one finds oneself quite on the crest of such a knife-edge, with one's feet well turned out, and one's axe almost useless from the absence of anything at the side to stick it into. From this ridge the eye plunged down direct to the Turtman glacier on the right, lying nearly 3000 feet below, and on the left to the Bies-glacier, from which rose the sharply pointed Weisshorn, while 10,000 feet lower than the ridge on which we stood, a silvery thread marked the course of the Visp between Stalden and St. Nicholas. The snow on the *arête* was in perfect condition, firm without being too hard, and seldom requiring the use of the axe. We kept as

much to the right as the extreme steepness of the
slope rendered possible, for we were anxious to keep
well off the cornice. Once we bore to the left, and
tried to ascend by the rocks, but the footholds were
so few and far between, and the *détours*, which
the difficulty of the rocks rendered desirable, were
so many, that we found it better to return to the
snow. Every step had to be made with care, and
it was seldom prudent for more than one of us to
move at a time. Thus more than two hours passed
before we were within measurable distance of the
summit. " Measurable distance," in climbing a
new peak, is invariably a very short distance, as,
until the last moment, it is seldom possible to know
what unexpected obstacles may be met with. At
last, however, we got off the snow, and began to
climb the rocky point which formed the summit of
the mountain. As Imboden placed his axe near
the top, the stone on which he put it slipped away,
and off went the axe, clattering down towards the
Bies-glacier. A step or two more and the peak
sunk to the rank of its surrounding brethren, and
what I believe to be the last but one unscaled
mountain, over 13,000 feet high, in the Alps, was

conquered. Not a sign of a previous ascent could
be discovered, so the peak was really ours. We
built the regulation stone man, deposited our names
in a bottle, and congratulated each other in no
measured language. Then, as we had a long descent
before us and the clouds had begun to boil up from
the valley, threatening a thunderstorm, we began
our downward way. The descent of the ridge was
easier than the ascent, owing to the good steps
which we had made while mounting ; but, for a
short distance, the steepness of the slope rendered it
advisable for us to go down, face inwards. It was a
real pleasure, on reaching our little possessions, left
further down, to examine the long *arête* with its
line of tracks along it, though we could only halt
for a few minutes, as the sky grew more and more
overcast. After descending the rocks for some time,
Imboden said that by bearing to the right, and gaining a snow slope, we should probably be able to get
down quicker, this slope joining the rocks further
below. Accordingly we traversed and began the
descent of this slope. Snow lay loosely over the
ice beneath, and, after a few steps, a loud " whish ! "
announced that the powdery substance had begun

to start off in an avalanche, and, in a few seconds, a broad streak of ice had been swept clear by it. Owing to the great heat the ice was by no means hard, and, the slope not being very steep, we found it easy to descend in the track of the avalanche ; we had had no difficulty in holding fast when it started just above us. The rocks were quickly reached, and then the snow slope below them had to be descended. We chose a place where the rocks came well down towards the glacier, and, as the snow was so extremely soft, we took the precaution, before trusting ourselves to it, of throwing down some large stones, in order that the snow, if it wished to form an avalanche, might do so before it had an opportunity of carrying us down with it. Once fairly on the snow, we made our way as fast as we could out of the reach of falling stones on to the plateau of the Bies-glacier, and trudged along towards the Biesjoch. On reaching that pass, snow began to fall lightly, but the heat was intense, and the snow on the Turtman glacier simply detestable. We sank to our waists at every step, and at last tried to advance on our knees, but were so over-come by the thought of what ludicrous objects we must be in that position, slowly advancing across the snow-field, that our laughter obliged us to resume a mode of progress enabling us to give all our attention to the avoidance of crevasses, for the strongest snow bridge would not have been safe in such heat. It took us an hour and a half to descend from the Biesjoch to the Bruneggjoch, a distance covered that morning in forty minutes' ascent, and we were glad of a little rest on rejoining our baggage on the pass. The question then arose as to how we should descend from there. If we took the route, followed in the ascent, we should reach Herbrigen, a small village from which we should have to walk to Randa, a distance of some miles, before we could get a carriage to take us to Zermatt. If, on the other hand, we crossed a stony point to our left (looking towards Zermatt), we should reach a pass between this point and the Inner Barrhorn, called the Barrjoch, and, crossing this pass, be able to descend to St. Nicholas, where we could sleep. We decided for the latter, as I was glad to have an opportunity of seeing more new ground. It was a very pretty pass ; a steep snow slope leading down beneath the cliffs of the Barrhorn, and bringing us

out on the fine glacier below. This glacier we
descended, and then bore away to the left, passing,
after an hour or so, below the Stellijoch, a pass
which forcibly reminded me of Tyrolese scenery,
with its bare, straight, regular walls of rock, between
which a glacier flowed down. As we crossed the
stony slopes, the thunder began to roll and our
axes to sing their responses in a somewhat disquieting manner. But the rain kept off till we reached
St. Nicholas at 8.30 p.m., and then it descended in
torrents. We returned to Zermatt next day.

CHAPTER VIII.

OVER THE MATTERHORN FROM VISP TO BREUIL,
AND BACK BY THE COL ST. THEODULE WITH-
OUT SLEEPING OUT.

The Matterhorn is irresistible—Alexander Burgener consents
to start at 11 p.m.—The hut is occupied by an American
and his guide, who have gone up to see the sunrise—
They are anxious to follow us up the Matterhorn—They
find holding on with their hands formidable work and
retire after five minutes of it—The summit of the
Matterhorn—Ice on the rocks—The ladder—Condition
of the Tyndal *arête*—Alexander calls for a halt till the
moon should rise—A weary descent—We are obliged
to cut steps down the whole of the glacier Du Lion—
Breuil—Alexander mounts a donkey—The Col St.
Théodule—Professor Schultz.

THOUGH the Matterhorn is so well known to
climbers that they are not likely to be interested
in hearing about it, yet it may perhaps amuse
some of my readers if I tell them of a passage I
made over this mountain.

On the morning of August 19th, 1883, I left Visp for Zermatt, walking as far as St. Nicholas and then driving. The weather was cloudless, and as the carriage turned the corner where the Matterhorn first becomes visible, its aspect as it shot upwards against the dark-blue sky was most inviting.

Strolling out into the garden of the Hotel Zermatt, after dinner that evening, the mountain, blotting out the stars with its wedge-like form, looked still more attractive, and I suddenly resolved that if I could find a good guide I would start to ascend it that very night. Having come to this decision, I hunted about for a long time in vain, receiving answers from all the best men to the effect that they were engaged. At last a friend caught sight of the dark face of Alexander Burgener, and asked him if he would go. He had that day crossed the Matterhorn with Professor Schultz. They started at an early hour from the hut on the Swiss side, went over to Italy, and returned by the Furgenjoch. It occurred to me, therefore, that Alexander had probably had enough exercise for the present. However, he thought otherwise, and told me that he would be ready to start by 11 p.m., and Professor Schultz, whose guide he was, having most kindly consented to let me take him, the matter was settled. I therefore went to my room about ten o'clock, arrayed myself in climbing garb, had supper, and punctually at eleven we set out.

A little before three we reached the hut, and went in in order to make some coffee, thereby rudely awakening from their slumbers an American and his guide, who had slept there to see the sunrise. The guide was very anxious to take his Herr up the Matterhorn, and kept on begging me in German to urge the American to make the attempt, Alexander meanwhile listening with a scowl of contempt on his face. I asked the traveller if he had made any previous ascent. "Oh dear, yes," he said, and mentioned some unfamiliar names of American hills, also the Gorner Grat. He then observed, surveying the mountain with a critical air, that any way he supposed it would not be more difficult to go to the summit than it had been to reach the hut, "for," he remarked, "to come up here we had even to hold on

with our hands in some places!" This decided
me to let them try it, for I was quite certain that
after five minutes' "holding on with their hands,"
they would find discretion the better part of valour.
Nor was I mistaken. We had taken but a very
few steps upwards when we saw our friend being
carefully let down on his back over a rock which was
more or less, but especially less, on a slope, and then
they were lost to sight. The climb to the summit
was trying, owing to the intense heat of the sun
beating straight on our backs. Once on the top a
cool breeze greeted us, and we spent an hour of
intense enjoyment looking at the magnificent view
around us, the distant mountains free from a trace
of cloud, and the pointed Viso standing like a
sentinel looking towards the plains of Lombardy.
No words can convey more than the faintest idea
of the charm of such a view seen on such a day.
Breuil lay far below. We did not intend to go
there, but to return, as Professor Schultz had done,
by the Furgenjoch.

Reluctantly I tore myself from the view, and
prepared for the gymnastics which I knew were in
store for us on the descent. There is not much

difficulty until one reaches the ladder. Here the real scrambling begins. The climber finds himself on a sloping slab of rock. In the centre of this slab two cords are seen side by side. They disappear at the edge, and the next objects which he sees on casting his eyes over the precipice are the pastures near Breuil, many thousand feet down. Below the rock these ropes form a ladder, which falls sheerly at first, and then is held back in a loop by its lower end being attached to the nearest point at which there is standing room. Consequently, as soon as the traveller is fairly on the ladder, it begins to swing with his weight, and the rungs not being directly below each other on account of its curved shape, much strain comes on the arms while the feet grope for the next step. A glance down should not be missed by the climber who is sure of his head, the sight is sensational in the extreme. When I was about half-way down the ladder I heard a loud exclamation from Alexander, and immediately after a block of ice flew over my head. It appeared that he had had one of his feet on it, and, owing to the heat of the rocks, the under part had melted and the whole piece slipped away.   As Alexander's power of balancing himself on next to nothing may be compared to those of Blondin, no harm ensued, but for one horrible instant I fully expected to see him also shooting down over the ledge.   There was a good deal of ice on the rocks, in a melting and unstable condition.   The long ridge called the Tyndall *arête* was covered on the top by three or four feet of snow, and the sun had been so powerful that very few of the tracks of Professor Schultz's party could be seen, owing to the melting of the snow. It was exceedingly unpleasant to walk in, as we had to make certain of our footing at each step, the soft substance sliding off continually in small, hissing avalanches.   Our progress was thus very slow, and it was dusk before we were fairly off the ridge.   " Well," said Alexander, " we can't go on in the dark ; the moon will rise in an hour ; till then we must wait here."   We were on a sort of platform, about three feet wide and a dozen long.   The guide and the porter sat down and slept, after tethering me and asking me to call them when it should be light enough to go on.   The cold was intense. At a distance water trickled down the rocks, but it was impossible to reach it. Our tea and wine and all our eatables were finished, and thirst began to inflict its tortures on us. I walked backwards and forwards along the ledge. Far away lay the plains of Lombardy covered with a slowly-rising mist. Through the curling vapour rose the Viso and other Alpine towers of silence, with the first shimmer of the moon on them. Higher she came, and the ice of the glacier began to glitter, and the black shadows to fall across the streams of light, and the slumbering valleys below to become visible and show to us at what a height we were above them.

I awoke Alexander and the porter, and we began once more our downward way. Sometimes I saw the beginning of a rope. Far below the porter's voice would be heard calling to me to come. Then I would turn my face inwards, take the cord in my hand, and, plunging into the deep shadow, grope my way down, Alexander often descending with the rope looped round a rock above him. Owing to the heat of the day and the melting of the snow, a film of ice covered many of the rocks. The shingle near the beginning of the

Couloir du Lion was transformed into a very slippery glacier, irritating beyond measure to walk down. As we approached the head of the Glacier du Lion, the moon sank, and again Alexander called for a halt. Once more I spent the time in pacing up and down till the grey light of early morning allowed us to set out again.

Then began the weary work of cutting steps down the glacier, which was frozen from top to bottom. With throats and tongues parched and swollen from thirst and fatigue, and eyes tired from constant watchfulness, we zigzagged down the slope, the silence of the mountain world only broken by the blows from the porter's axe as step after step was hewn, or by the distant roar of the stones which pour from time to time down the cliffs of the Matterhorn. It was still dusk when we reached a patch of rocks over which flowed a tiny stream. The delight with which we filled our drinking-cups can be imagined, and we went on again greatly refreshed after our draught of the somewhat muddy glacier water. It was 8 a.m. when we entered the hotel at Breuil, lack of provisions obliging us to descend to it instead of crossing back to Zermatt by the Furgenjoch. From Breuil there is a good bridle-path to within an hour of the Col St. Theodule. We determined to ride so far if any animals were forthcoming. Breakfast concluded, we were informed that there was a mule and also a donkey at our disposal. For some obscure reason the mule was assigned to me, and very comical was it to see Alexander's powerful form mounted on a creature hardly larger than himself. He and the porter took it in turns to repose their wearied limbs by riding the poor little donkey. Leaving the animals when the glacier was reached, we walked to the Col in an hour, and rested there for some time, the heat being so great. Then *en route* once more, and at 5.30 p.m. we entered the Monte Rosa at Zermatt.

I felt most guilty in having detained Professor Schultz's guide for so long, but he took the matter in the kindest way possible, and assured me that he had not been inconvenienced. Thus ended a period of continual exertion, lasting for forty-two and a half hours. Out of this time the guides had had two hours' sleep while I walked about to keep myself warm, but Alexander had been at work the whole of the day on the evening of which he started with me ; and I, on the other hand, had come on foot from Visp to St. Nicholas that morning, so we all had taken quite as much exercise as was good for us, to say the least of it.

CHAPTER IX.

THIRD ASCENT OF THE HIGHEST POINT OF THE DENT DU GÉANT.

A short account of the Dent du Géant—Signor Alessandro
Sella's ascent—Mr. Graham's ascent—We start for the
Col du Géant—State of the hut—A thunderstorm—Bad
weather obliges us to return—Mr. Hartley's ascent—
Our second attempt—Bad weather again—We console
ourselves by a scramble up La Vièrge—A fine day at
last—Burgener's cairn—Michel enjoys himself—The
first summit—Description of the climb from the lower
to the higher peak—The view—A furious wind—
Montanvert—Mr. Donkin's photograph of the Dent du
Géant.

SUCH numbers of English people visit Montanvert
every year that the sharply-pointed form of the
Dent du Géant must be familiar to many of them.
I will briefly mention a few facts in connection
with this peak. Many attempts were made to
scale it at different times. Charlet Stratton, a
Chamonix guide, who first reached the summit of

the Petit Dru, tried alone to find a way up the Dent du Géant. He examined the mountain on every side, and came to the conclusion that it was impossible to ascend it without artificial aid, as by fixing nails and ropes to the rocks. Alexander Burgener conducted a party as far as the lower part of some steeply sloping slabs. From this point further progress could not be made, and a small stone man was built, called Burgener's cairn.

Time passed on. One day in July, 1882, Edouard Cupelin was ascending Mont Malet, a peak not far from the Géant. When scrambling up some rocks near the summit (the climb being made by a new route) the porter exclaimed, " Look ! there is a flag on the Dent du Géant !" Cupelin, who, at that moment, was making a move upwards over a particularly steep and slippery piece of rock, told the porter with some warmth not to talk nonsense, but to attend to his work. The youth said no more for the time being, but, when the climbing became less severe, he again repeated his remark, adding, " Look, and see for yourself" Impatiently Cupelin turned to look, but no sooner

had he done so than he cried, " Ma foi ! C'est bien
vrai, cependant ! " and the party began to specu-
late with much eagerness who the happy person
was who had made the first ascent of the Géant.
It was noticed that the flag was fixed on what
appeared to be the lower of the two points, but
they were so nearly of a height that absolute
certainty could not be felt, nor, as it afterwards
was proved, did the circumstance of the inferior
height of that part of the mountain on which the
flag was placed in the least affect the credit due to
those who made this first ascent, since the difficulty in reaching the lower summit far surpasses
that found in passing from one point to the
other, the second peak exceeding the first in
height by about four or five feet only. The
next day it was known at Montanvert that Signor
Alessandro Sella, with Maquignaz as leading guide,
had accomplished the first ascent of the Dent du
Géant.

It was a work requiring both time and patience.
On many parts of the mountain ropes had to be
fixed and iron nails driven into the rock to attach
them to, as there was neither foot-hold nor hand-

hold. Maquignaz deserves the greatest credit for his engineering of the mountain. Signor A. Sella's ascent was followed by that of some more Italians. The ropes left by them were poor in quality, and by no means new. In the autumn of the same year Mr. Graham went up the peak, accompanied by the guides Auguste Cupelin and Payot. They reached the higher of the two points. I should have mentioned that the reason which induced Signor A. Sella to return without going up both peaks, was that, by the time he reached the place where his flag was planted, it was already very late in the afternoon, and every minute which remained of daylight was required for the descent. I state this on the authority of Signor Vittorio Sella, a cousin of Signor A. Sella.

My guide was very desirous of following in his brother's footsteps, and when I arrived at Montanvert in June, 1883, he suggested that we should take advantage of the first fine day to ascend the Géant. The weather that season was most unsettled. We waited day after day for the sky to clear sufficiently to give us a fair chance of attaining our object. At last, on the 28th, we set out for the Col du Géant. The air was extremely sultry, and when we reached the snow we found it so soft that we often sank to our knees. The guides were heavily loaded, as Cupelin insisted on taking a large supply of new rope to place as we went up the rocks by the side of the cords already there, for his brother Auguste had assured him that when he made the ascent with Mr. Graham in the autumn, the ropes were then much frayed and worn, and hanging all the winter was not likely to have improved them.

When we entered the hut we found that some hard work lay before us. The floor was covered with ice to a depth of several inches, and snow had penetrated through crevices in the walls, and altogether our quarters looked most comfortless. However, some one must be the first of the season to spend the night there, and, as we had plenty of time before us, it was rather amusing than otherwise to chop away the ice with our axes and shovel out the snow. Our party consisted of the brothers Cupelin and Michel Savioz. Two guides would have been sufficient, but during our winter climbs, on all of which Michel had accompanied me as

porter, he had so constantly spoken of the delight
it would give him to ascend the Géant, and his
hope that some one would take him up it before
long, that it was a real pleasure to me to let him
accompany us on this occasion, as a slight recom-
pense for the continual good-humour, willingness
to please and make himself useful, and pluck which
he showed during all our scrambles. Auguste
Tairraz was also with us, having helped to carry up
some of the ropes, provisions, and firewood for us.
It afterwards appeared that he was firmly resolved
to ascend the Géant instead of remaining at the
hut during our absence, and he had settled in his
own mind that, if we refused to take him, he would
go alone ! We had been working so hard in trying
to make our hotel comfortable that a loud crash of
thunder, followed by rolling echoes which pealed
amongst the surrounding peaks, caused us to start
and look out. While the men hastily brought in
our possessions, which had been left on the rocks
outside, I went to the edge of the cliff, from which,
looking over, Courmayeur can be seen, seven
thousand feet below. The sight was one of the
grandest I have ever witnessed. Far down black

K

clouds surged up and filled the valleys. Away to
the east one strip of pale blue sky was visible,
against which stood some of the Zermatt peaks,
white and calm and peaceful amid the howling
storm which already began to rage about their
feet. The heavens grew more and more angry-
looking, and streaks of crimson and indigo appeared
through the boiling mists. Soon the valleys were
buried in the seething mass, and only the long line
of Alpine sentinels, on the ridge of which I stood,
remained proud and untouched, looking down on
the confusion beneath while sunbeams played about
their heads. Again a roar of thunder and a
blinding flash of lightning.

" Come in ! " called the guides, and, as I returned
to the hut, the full force of the storm broke on the
ridge, and hail began to fall in stones as large as a
pigeon's egg. The clatter and noise were tremen-
dous. We could hardly hear each other speak.
The axes had long ago been placed outside, where
they could sing to their heart's content without
hurting any one, the musical talent displayed by an
ice axe during a thunderstorm being as wonderful as
it is disquieting. For some time the din of the

storm and the flashes of lightning occupied our
attention. Cupelin was the first to speak aloud
the thought which was, I fancy, in the minds of all
of us, "We shall have to return to Montanvert
to-morrow without ascending the Géant, I fear," he
remarked. Before nightfall the fury of the storm
had abated, but I can't say much for the degree
of comfort in which we spent the hours till morning.
There was about an inch of water on the floor of
the hut, owing to the melting of the ice which still
remained, despite all our efforts to get rid of it.
The furniture consisted of an extremely diminutive
table, some very narrow seats fastened along the
walls, and one plank ; this last article representing
the spring mattress of the establishment, and when
propped up by a stone under each end of it to keep
it out of the water, and placed across the hut, it
was assigned to me as my couch. I did not find it
everything which could be desired, owing to the
fact that, having once balanced myself along the
centre of it, the smallest movement disturbed the
equilibrium, and as I was once or twice so rash as
to indulge myself in a little sleep, I was generally
awakened by a sensation of extreme cold in one of

my feet, consequent on its having found a temporary resting-place in the lake. Two strings, with a few frayed threads attached to them, composed what I had been told was the great luxury of the place, namely, a hammock.

The next morning, as soon as it was light, we set out on our return to Montanvert. Snow was falling heavily, and the Géant was concealed by mist. We hid our ropes in the rocks of the Aiguilles Marbrées, and pitied ourselves greatly. So ended our first attempt on the Dent du Géant.

I will say only a few words concerning our second start for that mountain. It was particularly unfortunate. The weather was bad for some time, though there were occasionally single fine days. I consulted Cupelin on the advisability of making the ascent in one day from Montanvert. He thought that, as he had to fix the ropes during the climb, we should be delayed, and the time be too short, so he said that he would like to go the first fine day with his brother, put up the ropes, sleep that night at the cabin on the Col du Géant, and let Michel and me join him there about five o'clock next morning, if the weather still remained good.

This I agreed to, and on July 4th they started. I looked for them eagerly with a telescope at the time I thought them likely to become visible, and my surprise was very great when, after watching their two figures reach the upper part of the slabs, I noticed quite a little crowd standing near Burgener's cairn. This, I afterwards learnt, was a party, including Mr. Hartley and some other Englishmen, who had come up from Courmayeur.

That night, Michel and I departed on our weary trudge through the darkness to the Col. The sky was clear when we started, but gradually fleecy clouds crept over it, and, by the time that we were all fairly on the first slopes above the Col leading to the Géant, snow had begun to fall. Reluctantly, we retraced our steps, and consoled ourselves as best we could by a scramble up La Vièrge, which we fondly believed to have been, till then, unclimbed. All honours were paid to her, and a red cotton handkerchief belonging to Auguste, was tied to a rock on the summit. Then we went down to Montanvert, preaching patience to each other *en route.*

On the night of the 13th, we quitted the hotel

at Montanvert, bound for the third time for the Géant. The stars shone from a cloudless sky, and, as the sunrise tinged the snowy dome of Mont Blanc with pink, we emerged from amongst the shattered and tottering masses which form the ice fall of the Glacier du Géant. Our peak looked more sharply pointed than ever, seen through the clear atmosphere, and it was difficult to realize that we should, in a few hours, be standing on its summit. We breakfasted by the little stream which runs through the snow above the *séracs*, and then set out towards the Col. This time, we did not go to the hut, but crossed the snow-field below the Aiguilles Marbrées, steering straight for the slopes of the Géant. From this point, a long and tiresome climb landed us at the foot of the actual peak. Arrived there, we lunched and left the knapsacks, ice-axes, and everything which was not absolutely necessary, the guides turning out of their pockets a marvellous collection of surplus tobacco, candle-ends, old bits of bread, books of certificates, and other nondescript articles. The view was striking, as this part of the mountain overhangs the valley of Courmayeur.

Before starting for the real scramble of the day, our ninety feet of rope was attached to us in all its length, so that there was a considerable distance between each person. The party was arranged as follows :—Auguste Cupelin led, his brother came next, I was third, and Michel last. The climbing as far as Burgener's cairn is easy, but once there, the whole aspect of the mountain changes. Directly above, some smooth slabs of rock are placed at a considerable angle. They are smoothly polished, but are divided by a crack which runs down the centre of them. By the side of this crack, a rope has been fixed by means of a few iron nails, which have been placed wherever there is a crevice which will admit of their being driven in. Above these slabs the rock appears to rise in a sheer and un-broken wall, but as all other sides of the peak actually overhang, it is up the face of this cliff that the traveller must go. Nor is it as bad as it looks. There are no loose stones save one, which has been called the rocking-stone, and round which the rope passes in a loop. As the tension increases, the stone moves a little, which does not tend to steady the nerves of the climber, should he be

unaware of the fact that the stone is too firmly
jammed in to allow of its falling. The slabs were
decidedly pleasant to ascend, as each person goes
up directly above the other; this is always much
less trying than traversing. It is curious to watch
this part of the climb from Montanvert. The
travellers are almost against the sky-line, and only
part of their bodies can be seen, the crack con-
cealing the rest. They look, through the telescope,
like flies on a church spire, as they creep slowly up
the steep slabs.

As we ascended this part of the mountain, I
could hear Michel telling himself, with many ex-
clamations of delight, how much he was enjoying
the scramble, and the continual grin on his face
widened to an alarming extent whenever, as was
not unfrequently the case, he could find no resting-
place either for hands or feet. Altogether, he was
evidently having what our American cousins would
call "a real good time." Above the slabs
there is a ledge which must be followed for a little
distance. Here there is a cord which generally
forms a hand-rail, but on this occasion it was buried
in the fresh snow which was plastered up against

it. Then comes a short gulley, with an unpleasant amount of ice in it. Emerging from the gully, the work becomes easier till some more slabs are reached. These have to be traversed, and I thought the few steps across them the most difficult of the whole climb, as there really is hardly room for one or two nails in the side of one's boot, in the tiny ledges, and each step must be a long one. Then the rocking-stone is reached, and soon afterwards some perpendicular gullies. A fixed rope hangs down the centre of them, and the ascent of this passage is very fatiguing for the arms, as almost the whole weight of the body comes on them. It is a relief when a sort of shoulder, slightly projecting from the first peak, is reached. Here there is a place large enough for several persons to stand at ease before assaulting the last slope of the lower tooth. The flagstaff is not seen till one reaches this peak, but once there, all the rest of the route is in full view. The second peak is seen to be joined to the first by a sort of pass, consisting in a ridge which falls away sheerly to a depth of many thousand feet on either side. To reach this little Col, a descent of some forty feet or so must be

made. The peculiarity of this *arête* which thus
connects the two summits, consists in a hump of
rock perched on it which juts out on one side just
where the ridge must be struck. This obstacle has
to be passed round; it cannot, owing to the peculiar
formation of the ridge, be climbed over. Consequently, the traveller must clasp his arms round
it and grasp what he can with his left hand,
gradually worming himself in that direction.
Meanwhile, the man above has a firm footing (what
Cupelin would describe as "solide comme un
bœuf!"), and could easily check a slip, and there
is also good standing-room on the ridge for the
leading guide, so this awkward little passage is not
really dangerous or even very difficult, though it is
extremely uncomfortable. Once on the ridge, the
highest point is easily attained from there.

The actual summit consists of a flat slab of rock
perhaps six feet wide and as many long. No part
of the descent can be seen, except the lower peak,
as the rock falls away in vertical and, in some parts,
in overhanging walls on all sides.

We felt as if our platform floated in mid-air,
amongst the spires and domes of the great moun-

tains around, so completely did we seem to be separated from the earth below. Far down, the silent stream of the Mer de Glace flows onwards towards Montanvert. Lower still, on the other side of the range, the green fields and valleys, purple where the shadows fall, may be seen, backed by the pointed Grivola, Grand Paradis, and other peaks of the Graian Alps, and further still, if the eye could penetrate the rising mist, the cities of northern Italy, and the battle-field of Magenta might be observed. Even as our eyes ranged over the wonderful panorama spread round us, the clouds began to travel up, driven by a furious wind, and a rapid change in the weather was evidently not far distant.

We hastily prepared to quit the spot, which for so long we had looked forward eagerly to reaching, and hardly were we under weigh when snow began to fall, and the wind to howl and rage amongst the cliffs. We had often to stop on our downward way, and cling with all our force to the rocks, as the gusts of wind made frantic dashes at us, and seemed as if they would tear us from our insecure positions. A couple of hours sufficed for us to reach the place

where we had left the knapsacks, and then our
difficulties were over. A violent thunderstorm
came on soon after we had passed through the
séracs of the Géant, and we were drenched to the
skin by the time that the hospitable doors of
Montanvert opened to admit us.

An extremely successful photograph has been
taken by Mr. W. F. Donkin, of the higher peak of
the Dent du Géant, from the lower peak. The
enlargements from his negative are so striking
that an invalid friend of mine, seeing one of these
pictures hanging up in my sitting-room one
evening, had such a severe nervous attack in consequence of the impression it gave him of the
horrors of the peak, that a doctor had to be called
up during the night to administer remedies.

I recommend any of my readers who desire to
become better acquainted with this mountain
than I can make them by any verbal description,
to examine one of these photographs at Spooner's,
in the Strand. Taking a camera up such a peak
was, in itself, a wonderful feat.

A Street in Wiesen (Winter).

CHAPTER X.

PRIMITIVE CUSTOMS OF SOME ALPINE VILLAGES.

Wiesen in winter and spring—Result of a death in the village—Agriculture—Haymaking—Pontresina in winter —Treatment of criminals—The policeman—Education —Examination of porters at Chamonix who desire to become guides — Notice-boards—Advertisements— Wiesen again—Laws against riding, driving, and to-bogganning on certain days—The watchman—A village concert—A wedding—Excursions—A ball—Feats of strength—A digression in order to relate some amusing incidents of a winter stay in the heights—Bradshaw does his best to amuse the continental traveller.

IN order to learn the quaint customs of the inhabitants of some of the small Alpine villages, one must live in them at all seasons of the year, but more especially during the months when strangers do not travel. It is also necessary to gain the confidence of the natives, and to be on very friendly terms with them, encouraging them to speak of their local affairs, and taking an interest in all that concerns them.

I have lived, during all last winter, in the little village of Wiesen, in the Canton of the Grisons. This lovely place is known in summer principally to Swiss and Germans, but until 1884-85 it had not been frequented in winter. During the winter mentioned, however, five English people stayed there, and last season there were about twenty winter guests. The climate is milder than that of Davos, and, when the snow begins to melt, the drying of the roads takes place very quickly, owing to the steepness of the slope on which the village is built. Wiesen is 4771 feet above the level of the sea, and about a thousand above the river. The scenery all round is magnificent, and in spring the landscape becomes fairy-like in its beauty. The slopes are studded with blue gentians and lilies of the valley, and woods of larch and pine clothe the hill-sides, while above, the glaciers of Piz d'Aela glitter and shine, and the Tinzenhorn and Piz Michel stand as sentinels on the chain which separates the valley of the Landwasser from the Engadine.

Wiesen is reached in six hours from Chur, and

in an hour and a half from Davos. The villagers are very simple in their ideas, and some of their customs are excessively curious and primitive.

It sometimes happens that one of the peasants by reason of extreme old age, dies. The whole population of the village at once clothes itself in black, and continues to wear mourning for three weeks. Perhaps this custom may have originated in the fact that, in so small a community, each person is related in a more or less distant degree to every one else. The peasants, though very poor, are not in actual want, but great thrift is necessary for them to gain enough to keep them. Wages are very low, the women receiving seven pence (70 centimes), and their food, for working in the fields from six o'clock in the morning till dusk, while the men make fifteen pence (1 franc 50 centimes), and often less, their food being also given them.

The soil is very poor and, in some places, so thin that the rock is reached at a depth of a foot or less below the surface. Owing to the excessively steep slope of the ground near Wiesen, the earth slips down during the year to a considerable extent, and, in order that the upper parts may not become quite bare, the following method of keeping up the soil is resorted to. A post is driven into the ground at the top of the slope. To this post a pulley is fastened, with a rope of platted hide passed round it. A wheelbarrow is attached to each end of the rope, and, as one of the labourers descends, he pulls up the man who is mounting, whose barrow is filled with soil from a trench dug along the bottom of the field. This soil is put above, and thus replaces the earth which has slipped gradually down. The land must be treated in this way every year, thereby adding another to the many difficulties of cultivating the fields in the mountainous districts of Switzerland.

In spring the land is ploughed. To accomplish this four cows are required. As very few families possess so many, they unite together, and perhaps each family contributes one. Then they go and work on the field belonging to the owner of one of the cows, and when that is finished, pass on to the next, and so on till all is done, the whole of the four families joining in the work. The cows are

guided by a child, who walks in front and flicks
them on their noses with a switch, when they have
to turn at the end of a furrow. Two ploughs are
used, each drawn by a pair of cows. The first
breaks up the ground, and the second, following
immediately after, turns it over and makes the
furrow. Then some women break up the clods
with hoes, and a man walks after them, carrying a
bag of seed, which he scatters with his hand. The
final operation consists in raking the ground, in
order that the seed may be covered. In the
evening, when the day's work is over, the different
families may be seen returning home, carrying
their ploughs on their shoulders.

In hay-making time the peasants again turn out
in families, and, in some places, where the ground
is extremely steep, the danger of a slip is so great
that the hay-makers are roped. This can be seen
every autumn on the slopes below the Cap de
Moine, near Les Avants. The peasants are usually
very peaceable and honest, but of course now and
then a crime, generally on a very small scale, is com-
mitted. As a rule there is a place for locking up
prisoners in the villages, constructed in the most

L

primitive manner possible, regular prisons being
only found in the towns.

The subject of prisons recalls to me some
amusing anecdotes related by a friend who has,
for many years, been a constant visitor to Pontresina. It appears that whenever it is necessary
to lock up an evil-doer at Pontresina, it is the
custom to confine him in a room in the school-
house. Some time ago an Italian was sentenced
to a short term of imprisonment for stealing a
pocket-handkerchief. Feeling very thirsty in the
night, he took out his knife, screwed off the lock
of the door, and going downstairs, knocked at the
schoolmaster's door to beg for a glass of water.
This unsuspicious individual gave it to him, and
on the man's promising to return to his cell, he
went to sleep again. The Italian, having got what
he wanted, went back to his room, and proceeded
to screw the lock on again. In the morning he
was still in confinement, no doubt considering it
a luxury to have a bed to·sleep on, good food to
eat, and no work to do for several days.

Last winter an Italian stole two watches and
was placed in the same room, but he preferred

pushing the bars of the prison window aside and letting himself down to the ground by a rope made out of the bedclothes, in preference to disturbing the schoolmaster. This may be accounted for by the prisoner's being "wanted" in Italy for half-murdering his wife. Another curious custom is that, at the end of the visitors' season, the street lamps are dismantled, and the village policeman is sent away to visit Pontresina only once a month during the winter, just to see if any one wants to be taken up. This official makes up for his lack of work in winter by great activity in summer. The fact may be accounted for, when it is remembered that he receives half the fines inflicted on persons who walk on the grass, thereby injuring the hay, or otherwise transgress the laws. He carries a book containing various statutes, and, if he spies a nurse and children, of peculiarly inoffensive aspect, sitting innocently on the grass, he marches up to them, and, taking the book from his pocket, proceeds to read out the law relating to their offence. Having concluded, he holds out his hand for the fine, but the offenders, being English, and not having understood a word of what he has read to them, are completely mystified, evidently taking him for a skirmisher of the Salvation Army, and simply shake their heads, whereupon the policeman begins again, and once more reads the paragraph from beginning to end, this performance occasionally continuing for some time.

The winter is the season devoted to education, and the society at Pontresina, for keeping the paths and ways in order, procured some free instruction in geology for the guides a year or two ago, in order that when making excursions in summer with travellers their conversation might be more interesting, and that their minds might be improved by a wider range of knowledge. A geologist from Sils came over to give them lessons, and at one of the classes he stated, with some pride, that he would send a large parcel of stones, which he himself had collected, the next day by post from Sils to Pontresina. An old guide sitting by, whose conservatism is well known, and whose identity will be at once recognized by frequenters of Pontresina, raising his hand and pointing towards the mountains, remarked in tones of much scorn, "Stones! send *stones* by post! Why we have more stones than we know what to do with up the slopes behind the village! I've been up many a mountain without all this useless knowledge! Show me any man who will go up a peak better because he can talk about stones!" *Apropos* of the wish to raise the standard of education amongst guides, it may amuse my readers to hear the answers given by some Chamonix porters at an examination held in that village for the purpose of finding out whether several young men, who had till then acted as porters were eligible for reception into the society of guides. I quote from notes made on the spot.

Examiner.—"How do you know where the north is?"

Porter.—"By the sun being there."

Examiner.—"What is Switzerland?"

Porter.—"A kingdom."

Examiner.—"How would you cross the crevasse often found between a glacier and a moraine?"

Porter.—"By stepping over."

Examiner.—"But if it is very wide?"

Porter.—"Build a bridge across."

Examiner.—" Nonsense ! "

Porter.—" Go home again ? "

Examiner.—" *Never !* Cut steps, of course. Now, tell me what you would do if a traveller who was with you was very cold and tired, and wanted to go to sleep on a glacier ? "

Porter.—" I would tell him not to."

Examiner.—" But if he insisted ? "

Porter.—" Then I would beat him."

The examiner did not seem to think these answers unusual, and the candidate passed. But to return to Pontresina.

The troops of English who visit this place in summer do not appear to have imparted much skill in their language to its inhabitants, judging from the wording of some of the notice-boards. We are informed, when we enter some of the woods, that " In the months of July and August it will cuttered the wood in the forest. Because by the transport thereof stones are coming down, it is necessary to have care to it." While speaking of the frequent mutilation our language receives at the hands of foreigners, I must also mention the notices posted up in a hotel not five miles from

Pontresina. On the door of the salon we read "Dogs will by all means be chased from public rooms," and "To prevent disagreeableness and reclamation for lunchon and diner *table d'hôte* visitors are highly requested to be at the appointed tims." A leading article in the organ of that town began, "Why those hills of shadow tint appear more sweet than all the landscapes smiling near this distance lends enchantment to the view."

Though it relates to Italy and not to Switzerland, I cannot forbear adding one more extremely amusing notice. I copied it from an advertisement posted up at the railway station at Bordighera. Here it is :—

"I beg to inform travelling people that I have established a first class Hôtel at Arengano, 40 minutes from Pegli, Riviera di Ponente. This house, situeted suth, sorrownded by a beautiful oranges gardens—has a splendid view upon the coast till Genoa reparated from the north windy and wery kealthy. There finds the all beautiful, viz., a very swit climate by all season, a very good service, ecc., ecc.

" The actual master is the same Mrs. woho kept
the Hôtel d'Angleterre à Pegli."

The Swiss health resort which is famed for "its
dustless atmosphere and extraordinary frequency
of tourists," while "the hotel is furnished with
balconies and extensive views," does not compare
in the quaintness with which the advertisement is
worded with that recommending the establishment kept by the " Mrs." who owned the Angleterre
at Pegli.

But to return to Wiesen and its unsophisticated
inhabitants. Some of the laws, which I believe are
in force in all the towns and villages in that part of
the world, seem very autocratic to strangers. For
instance, there are three days in the year, Christmas
Day, Easter Day, and Harvest Thanksgiving Day,
on which no one but the pastor and the doctor is
allowed to ride, drive or toboggan. Each able-
bodied man in the commune is obliged to work on
the roads for a certain number of days every year,
unless he prefers to pay for a substitute. After a
heavy snowfall, nearly the whole village turns out
to open the communication and make the roads
practicable for sledges ; and, in the spring, when

some parts of the road are free from snow, before the old winter drifts have melted in other places, large parties of men and women spend their time, from sunrise to sunset, in breaking the hard-frozen substance and shovelling it off the road, where it quickly dissolves, and thus the track is prepared for wheeled vehicles. Wiesen, like Pontresina, is very quiet and peaceable in winter, and the police-man divides himself between Wiesen and Filisur, a village about six miles distant by carriage-road. There is, however, an official in each village, whose duty it is to look after the safety of the inhabitants. I made this person's acquaintance for the first time one night in spring, while spending a few weeks at Wiesen. I was awakened about midnight by a terrible noise under my window. It might have been shouting or it might have been quarelling, in any case it made the night hideous, and, as the sounds died away at length in the distance, I determined that I would speak my mind to Mr. Palmy, the hotel-keeper, and beg him to have the disturber of my slumbers restrained.

"Mr. Palmy," I remarked next morning, " there was a very disorderly person making a great noise under my window late last night ; he ought not to be allowed to wander about and make such a commotion at that hour !"

" What time was it ? " Mr. Palmy inquired.

" About midnight, I think," was my reply.

" Then," said Mr. Palmy, " it must have been *the watchman !* "

" The watchman ! " I exclaimed ; " but why does he make such a noise ? "

" Oh, he sings," Mr. Palmy replied.

" Does he ? " I inquired, somewhat sceptically. " Do you know the words of his song ? "

" Yes," said Mr. Palmy, " this is the verse he sings at midnight—

> " Hört, Ihr Herren, und lasst Euch sagen,
> Unsere Glock hat Zwölf geschlagen,
> Zwölf das ist die End der Zeit ;
> Mensch bedenk der Ewigkeit." [1]

" One would think of ' the end of time ' on hearing him sing," I observed, " even without under-

---

[1] " Hear, my masters, let me tell,
Twelve has sounded from our bell,
Twelve, which is of time the end,
Bids you think what road you wend."

standing the words ; anything more appalling I never had the misfortune to hear ! "

Mr. Palmy then told me that the watch is kept by a different person each month, all the villagers taking it in turn to fulfil this duty. Fortunately, the individual with the remarkable voice who disturbed me so much seems to combine strength of lungs and originality of execution to an extent not shared by his neighbours, not a few of whom are really musical, and when a monster concert is given at Alveneu by the choirs of the neighbouring villages, much of the singing is very good indeed.

A wedding in one of these little villages is a curious sight. The bride is always dressed in black, and, on her head, she wears a wreath of orange blossoms, from the back of which a long pig-tail of the same flowers hangs below her waist. Those of the wedding guests who wish to do much honour to the occasion, also appear in black, and after the ceremony, which closely resembles our own, it is not uncommon to see the bride start off for a long walk, accompanied by a number of her friends, while the bridegroom remains at home with the other men. A dance takes place in the evening, and the festivities are kept up during the greater part of the night. I have often wondered how the youths of Wiesen manage to propose for their wives ; one never sees the men and women together. On Sundays, before service, they wait outside the church in two separate parties, and on the arrival of the pastor, ready dressed in his black gown, they all flock into the building after him and take their places on different sides of the aisle. They never walk together, and, when working in the fields, the women invariably keep in one group and the men in another.

Three excursions are made during the winter in sledges. They take place on Sundays, and one of them is participated in only by the couples who have become engaged during the past year, another by those married within that time, and the third is undertaken by all the young people of the village, the men paying for the sledges. Each sledge holds two persons, the composition of the pairs being determined by lot.

Dancing is indulged in to a great extent in the winter months. The ball begins usually at two

The old Village of Wiesen in Winter

Page 180.

o'clock in the afternoon. At six o'clock dinner is partaken of, each girl bringing cakes and bread for herself and her partner, and the young men supplying coffee and wine. Dancing is continued after dinner, and goes on the entire night, the entertainment not concluding until seven o'clock next morning. Instead of going home and resting after all this exercise, the men spend an hour or two after the ball in feats of strength. Some of these trials of strength consist in two men sitting one on each side of a table, who clasp their right hands. Each man then pushes to his left, and whoever draws down his opponent's hand to the table is the winner. Again, two men placing themselves as above, lock the second fingers of their right hands together, and try who can pull the hardest; sometimes neither will give in till one or the other dislocates a finger. Another of these feats, in which also two men sitting on each side of a table engage, is this. The competitors place the elbow of the right arm on the table, then closing their hands, they press the outside of the fingers, from the knuckles to the central joints, against each other, and push as hard as possible, each endeavouring to force his opponent's hand off the table, and they will not unfrequently refuse to accept defeat till most of the skin has been rubbed off their fingers.

At a certain well-known hotel in the Canton of the Grisons, there was once upon a time a secretary who was very proud of his knowledge of English. Any orders which were given to him in that language had a curious way of not being carried out, but as he always replied, "Yes, sir, I quite understand," whenever he was told anything, it did not seem at first as if want of comprehension had anything to do with it.

One day an English clergyman, staying in the hotel, asked the secretary if he could get four Oxford frames for him, and went on to say, "Probably you don't know what Oxford frames are like ; I can show you some to give you an idea."

"Yes, sir, I quite understand what you want," the secretary replied, as usual.

A few days later the hotel-keeper, meeting the visitor who had ordered the Oxford frames, said to him,—

"My secretary tells me, sir, that you have requested him to procure you four oxen. I am afraid we can only supply you with one at present, but the other three shall be forthcoming in a day or two."

An English lady, asking the Swiss doctor in one of these Alpine health-resorts, if he could recommend her a cook, was greatly amused when he answered, "I find it much easier to become a wife than to become a cook in these places!" This unfortunate German word *bekommen* (to get) is very often translated into "become" by persons who have an imperfect knowledge of English, and I have heard a friend plaintively observing at a railway station, that she found it quite impossible to "become" her luggage!

The same Swiss doctor whom I have mentioned above, was heard regretting last winter that the lung of one of his patients was "very sensible (*sensitive*) in taking cold so easily."

And now a few words about that out-of-the-way little place, Jenisberg, the tiny village across the valley, which can only be approached on foot, in an hour's walking from Wiesen.

Jenisberg has its spiritual wants supplied by the pastor from its neighbour opposite, who goes over once *a year* to hold a service. It seems curious that it should possess a church which is so seldom made use of. This annual service takes place during the summer, when most of the peasants are on the Alps high above the village with their cattle. It is not too far for them to come down to attend church at Jenisberg, but they would not have time to pilgrimage over to Wiesen as they do during the winter. The baptisms and weddings, however, take place at the larger village, and the babies who come to be christened are often so swathed in garments and covered with veils, that, on at least one occasion, a child was found to have been smothered *en route*, the parents not understanding that lack of air could possibly be injurious.

The pastors of some of these villages have an easy, and for Switzerland, a luxurious life. The minister at Wiesen holds a service at Filisur on alternate Sundays, and also is obliged to go, as stated above, once a year to Jenisberg. For the fulfilment of these duties he receives a salary of £120 a year, a house, a supply of wood, which the

Grand Moulin, Morteratsch Glacier.

peasants take it in turns to cut up for him, and as many sacks of potatoes as he is likely to require. He has a little garden, and devotes a good deal of his time to his bees, and may often be seen visiting the hives with a sieve over his face, round which sacking is sewn, which covers his head and neck, and preserves him from any risk of stings.

But this chapter has quite overrun the limits, which even the most indulgent of my readers would be likely to prescribe as sufficient for one set of subjects, so I will try and tell them about something quite different in the next few pages, finishing this chapter with a piece of information taken verbatim from "Bradshaw's Continental Guide" (May, 1885), page 147.

"The Tête-Noire is one of the most picturesque passes in Switzerland, has a museum, baths, and a spire church, where a priory was founded in the eleventh century."

Truly, the Tête-Noire must be a remarkable pass!

Until some months ago travellers were informed by the same guide, that there was a diligence from Visp to Zermatt, and, turning to the pages devoted

M

to a time-table of the Swiss posts, the hour of starting of this phantom conveyance could be found. I have often wondered what the feeling of unsuspecting tourists would be on arriving at Visp, with a large supply of American trunks, at the sight of the "diligence," which consists of one or two baggage-mules, or sometimes, I believe, only of the postman.

But the immense accumulation of information which "Bradshaw's Guide" gives us, is too valuable for its editor not to have merited our warm thanks and admiration.

VILLAGE CHILDREN AT WIESEN TOBOGGANNING.

CHAPTER XI.

THREE VERY SMALL SCRAMBLES.

The Riffelhorn from the glacier—We decide to descend by
the same route—Imseng distinguishes himself. The
last gully—We make the descent—Guides who chuckle
reassuringly—Advantages and disadvantages of Pontresina in summer—"The Sisters"—Christian Grass—
Zermatt again—We start for the Rothhorn—Mist—We
go up the Unter Gabelhorn from the Triftthal—Dr.
Mosely's gully.

MANY of my readers have been, I am quite sure,
to the Gorner Grat, passing on the right the little
Riffelhorn. And, no doubt, a great number of
those who have visited the former point of view,
have also scrambled up the latter. The Riffelhorn
must therefore be familiar to not a few, and those
who know it by sight as well as those who have
climbed it, may be interested in hearing how we
made what seems to have been the first descent of

that part of the mountain commonly known as the route from the glacier.

The weather for some time had been very unpromising, but the Riffelhorn is always a good object for a walk whenever the higher peaks are concealed by clouds.

I had so often been up the Riffelhorn by the ordinary route, that I eagerly caught at the suggestion of a friend that we should go up from the glacier. We set out one morning with the object of making this excursion, and my friend had Peter Taugwalder as his guide, while I was accompanied by Abraham Imseng. The latter volunteered to take us straight up from the glacier by a route which seemed to be more in his brain than on the mountain, for, after leaving us spread out like limpets on some steep glacier-polished rocks, he went on to explore. While we waited he contrived to wriggle himself into a position from which he could neither move up nor down, and he was obliged to call Peter to his aid, the latter passing us with some difficulty, as we adhered as best we could to the slippery face of rock. As soon as Imseng was dislodged, we all went down again to the glacier and tried once more further back. Here the rocks were more broken, and, after mounting them for a little time, we reached the foot of the gully, up which we had to go. We sat down and lunched there, as the afternoon was getting on, our walk up the glacier, which we had taken in preference to the path by the Riffel, having consumed some hours. But we were in no hurry, as the charm of the work before us lay in its quality, rather than in its quantity.

After halting for half an hour or so, the two guides began a series of wonderful gymnastics on the rocks above. First, Imseng struggled a little way up, with some prodding and much verbal encouragement from Peter. Then, finding that grasping a rock with both arms and kicking his toes against upright slabs where no foothold existed, did not facilitate his ascent or allay the growing impatience of the guide below, he suddenly let go and subsided with a long slip and a clatter amongst the stones beneath. Then Peter made an attempt, but without any more satisfactory results.

Finally, Imseng gave up in despair, and bearing

to the left, found an easy passage, by mounting which he reached the upper part of the gulley. Settling himself comfortably and securely amongst the rocks, he threw down the loose end of the rope, which was caught by Peter, and then our share in the work began, Peter directing us from below. I was the first to start. A good pull at a projecting rock brought me into a place resembling a chimney, from which one side had been broken away, while three remained standing. In this *cheminée* large icicles had formed and hung all round. Obeying Peter's orders, I placed my feet on the little ledges which are most conveniently placed here and there for a short distance up it. Then the rock overhangs and the *cheminée* must be quitted, and some slabs to the left gained. This is the difficult bit. As the climber leans over, the rope also drawing him in the same direction, he feels as if a touch from a feather would disturb his equilibrium and turn him over, in which case he would find himself lying on his back on a smooth, steep slab, with his feet dangling helplessly over the precipice, and he himself only kept in position by the guide above who holds the rope, but from whom he is completely hidden, so that a sudden pull or letting out may be expected at any moment as an encouragement to come on, which the poor traveller is, of course, quite unable to do. Therefore, as far as I can remember, as soon as I had partly reached the slabs, Peter shouted to me to pass the rope to my right side (it was then at my back), and this I did by slipping myself along under it. Directly I had a firm hold of it the rest was easy, and, before long, I had joined Imseng, and was undoing the end of the rope which was tied round my waist, in order to throw it down to my companion. He climbed up with ease, Peter followed, and in a minute or two we all stood on the summit of the Riffelhorn.

Having compared notes as to our various sensations coming up, we began to prepare for the scramble down again. One of the guides, I think it was Peter, was the first to be launched, and judging from the number of times he called out to Imseng not to let the rope out so fast, he was evidently having a lively time of it, for it was, of course, much more difficult for the first man, as he had no one to direct him and tell him when he was near a foothold. At length the check on the rope ceased, and Imseng drew it up and attached my friend, sending him forth in a way which resembled the action of a fisherman throwing his bait. This time, things appeared to go more easily, and I was encouraged for my attempt by the information, which was shouted to me from below, that " it is all right as long as you don't let yourself turn over on your back ! " Tied in my turn to the free end of the rope, I departed on my knees. The one awkward little bit was got over more easily than I had expected, and soon I was wedged in the *cheminée.* While taking the last few downward steps, I was somewhat startled when all the ninety feet of rope arrived in a bundle from above, alighting just between me and my companions, and Imseng's eternal chuckle was faintly heard from overhead, as he left his post and started for the descent by the ordinary route. Cheerfulness in guides is a quality I much admire, and when their cheerfulness is of the kind displayed to per-fection by Peter Dangl, it tends to raise one's spirits ; but if, on remarking to a guide that one wishes he would be quick, as the ice-pinnacles above look very shaky, his response is to stop and giggle, then I consider his cheerfulness exasperating to the last degree, for I think that there is nothing so trying in risky positions as a reassuring chuckle. Imseng is a good guide, and, I am sure, an excellent person in every way, but I do wish that he would reform his habit of chuckling at moments when it is by no means *à propos*.

Now, I must ask you to travel with me up the Rhone Valley, across the Furka Pass and the Oberalp to Chur, and thence to the Engadine.

The Engadine in summer is crowded to overflowing by our compatriots, and, for some obscure reason, many of those who go there return to it year after year. The air is certainly magnificent, though not finer than that of Saas-Fée. The scenery, too, is beautiful, but I cannot admit that it will compare with the Riffel Alp, Fée, Bel Alp, or many other places. The hotels are overcrowded, and their proprietors, as a rule, independent and disobliging. I do not care to stay in a place where, if I complain of the food, I am liable to be told that my rooms are required for the following day.

For invalids, the Engadine has the advantage of being easy of access, owing to its carriage-road, of having a climate free from the mists which most places situated on hill-sides are more or less liable to, of good doctors, of short, level and shady walks, and plenty of society to amuse those who are not strong enough to walk far.

But the more robust will naturally prefer other hunting-grounds, where the mountains are finer, the hotel-keepers anxious to make travellers comfortable, and the majority of the guides neither extortionate in their charges, nor ignorant of all peaks and passes except those in their own district.

I had heard so much of the charms of the Engadine in summer, that I wished to visit it at that season, and one July, when the weather was fine, and Pontresina, as usual, crowded with people, I found myself there.

Most of my walks that summer were quite uneventful, so I shall only speak of one, which was amusing to us who took part in it, and possibly a very short description of it may recall a pleasant scramble to my readers, many of whom have doubtless made the excursion.

The Westerly Peak of the Two Sisters, from the Easterly Peak.

Young Christian Grass, an excellent little Pontresina guide, scrambled with me one day, soon after my arrival, over the peaks of the Two Sisters, As we stood on the summit of the lower or easterly point, I was much struck by the appearance of the highest, or westerly "sister." The walls of rock on the side facing us looked too unbroken to admit of their being climbed without very great difficulty, and the view of the precipitous and sharply-pointed peak, with St. Moritz and its lake, and the range of Piz Ot behind the Engadine valley forming the background, was very impressive.

"I wish we had the camera with us," Christian remarked to me, as we discussed the view in front of us; "we might come back another day, and then you could take a photograph from here," he added.

This suggestion was a good one, and I decided to act on it, our reason for having left the camera at home on this occasion, being the uncertainty of the weather, which was very cloudy when we set out.

A short time afterwards, meeting a friend who

was anxious to ascend " The Sisters," we agreed to
make the excursion together, and another friend
also deciding to join us with her guide, we settled
to start the following morning, the two guides
undertaking to look after the three travellers.

But just as Miss S. and myself, with Christian
Grass, were about to set out, a little note came
from our mutual friend, telling us that, as she
intended to start that night for Piz Roseg, she
feared to over-fatigue herself if she ascended " The
Sisters " in the morning. We were therefore left
with Christian as our sole guide, and as he had one
lady to conduct up the peak who had never set
foot on a mountain before, another who finds it
all she can do on rocks to look after herself, and,
worse than all, he was obliged to carry the
camera sticks, and prevent them from getting
jammed into gullies and hooked on to projecting rocks, I think that his hands were pretty
full. He shared my opinion, but engaged to
get us all up somehow in time. Arriving on
the little Col between the easterly peak of
" The Sisters " and Piz Murigal, the rope was
put on. Having expected our friend to bring

another long enough for three people, Christian
had only with him a cord of sufficient length for
two, and as his mind was much disquieted by
seeing me following unroped, I respected his
feelings, and wedged myself in between two rocks,
solemnly promising not to move till he should
return from taking Miss S. and the camera to the
top of the first peak. Miss S. went very well
indeed, but not so the tripod, for, in some places,
Christian found it more convenient to push it up
in front of him, leaving it on a ledge till he could
give it another lift on. Reaching the summit,
Miss S. and the camera were deposited in a safe
place, and down little Christian scrambled to my
nook. As soon as I had joined Miss S., Christian
suggested that they should begin their climb to
the other peak, while I arranged the camera and
got everything ready for taking a picture. I
wished to have their figures in it, as this would
increase the interest of the photograph, and give
an idea of the size of the mountain. It was curious
to watch them as they gradually mounted the
wall of rock in front, and one realized how extremely
deceptive its appearance of difficulty was, by the

ease with which they rose, step by step. As they reached a shoulder which projects to the left, and stood out against the sky line, I clapped my hands. This was the signal agreed upon, and they at once remained still. I made an exposure and released them from their position by again clapping my hands. As soon as they arrived on the summit I again photographed them. The view turned out to be the best taken that day, and when enlarged by the Autotype Company it really made a very effective picture. Christian was much pleased with what I fancy he looked upon as our joint production, and placed the copy which I gave him in a place of honour in his house. If the climb up "The Sisters," from the Col to the summit of the second point was a matter of three hours, instead of less than a sixth of that time, it would be one of the most delightful scrambles in Switzerland. As it is, the excursion is one which all who are not subject to giddiness and who like climbing, will thoroughly enjoy. Now let us return to Zermatt.

A year or two ago, a party, including two Englishmen, myself, and the guides Edouard

Cupelin, Imseng, Peter Taugwalder, and a porter, arranged to cross to Zinal over the Rothhorn, and back by the Moming or one of the other passes.

One starlight night we set out and trudged up the Triftthal, towards the snowy ridge by which the Rothhorn is approached. But the weather was not amiably disposed towards us, and, as the grey light of early dawn crept over the sky, a film of cloud began to veil the peaks, and, before long, our mountain was wrapped in mist, and snow had evidently begun to fall on the higher summits.

It was therefore quite useless for us to try and go over the Rothhorn, and, as the idea of returning to Zerm tt about four o'clock in the morning was not pleasant to us, we looked about and considered what employment, suitable to the state of the weather, could be found in the neighbourhood of the Triftthal.

The Unter Gabelhorn looks well from this side, and we inquired if any one had ever been up it from the direction of the Trift. The guides replied that they believed not, but they expressed their willingness to make an attempt from there if we wished to try it. It seemed the only piece of climbing to be had, so we determined to steer straight up for the ridge, and then work along to the right towards the summit.   But first the porter was sent back to Zermatt with such of our possessions as we did not require, and, whenever I think of the events of that day, I am much amused by recalling the comical aspect under which Cupelin appeared, as he stood in the faint light of dawn, the lantern still burning, in the wild, bleak Triftthal, engaged in counting, and mentally taking a list of the various articles, such as handkerchiefs, for instance, belonging to me which the porter was placing in his knapsack to take back.   When I travel with Cupelin, I invariably leave all the responsibility of packing and seeing that nothing is left behind, to him, and he takes upon himself so completely the united duties of courier, ladies' maid, guide, cook, and many other vocations, that he looks after all articles likely to go astray, as if that was the sole business of his life.

The surplus luggage disposed of, we began to ascend, each one straggling up by whatever route seemed best to him.   It was a tiresome walk, over loose stones, and the monotony was becoming trying when one of the party, who was slightly in advance of the others, managed to disturb the equilibrium of a rock about the size of a grand piano. He contrived to step aside as the great mass lurched over, and it can be imagined with what promptitude we, who were below, retired from what seemed the likely course of the huge boulder. Down it came, springing with deafening crashes from side to side, while the air became tainted with an odour of splintered flint. At last it reached the bottom of the slope, and we congratulated ourselves that no one had been struck, an event which would certainly have been fatal to the person receiving the blow.

On reaching the ridge the guides considered it advisable to rope us. The weather had been gradually getting worse and worse, and now a raging wind was blowing and driving a mixture of rain and snow into our faces. But the summit was near at hand, so setting to work with a will, we scrambled upwards and gained the foot of a steep and smooth gully overhanging the Triftthal, which led to the top of the peak. Peter was leading, and spent a considerable time in trying to wriggle

N

himself up this gully. Then Imseng made an
attempt, but though easy enough for a tall man,
the passage was decidedly difficult for those of
moderate height, as a good handhold near the top
of it was just out of their reach. Cupelin was the
third to try and ascend, and putting his feet as
high up as possible, he stretched out his six feet
four of height, and, grasping a projecting piece of
rock far up in the gully, found himself before long
on the summit. It was easy for us to join him by
aid of the rope, and, in a few minutes, we were all
gathered amongst the shattered blocks which form
the highest point of the Unter Gabelhorn. The
weather obliged us to curtail our stay there to a
very few minutes, and then we began the descent
by the ordinary route, which is quite easy, not
requiring the use of the rope. On returning to
Zermatt we made inquiries as to the history of
the Unter Gabelhorn, and, as far as we could as-
certain, our ascent was the second by the gulley
overhanging the Triftthal, the first ascent having
been made by Dr. Mosely, who was afterwards
killed on the Matterhorn. The Unter Gabelhorn
can also be ascended from the Triftthal, and our

gulley avoided, by traversing the peak to the left as soon as the travellers are fairly on the ridge at the foot of it. The ordinary route is thus joined a short distance below the summit.

CHAPTER XII.

TWO OLD FRIENDS.

Imboden makes a suggestion—Appearance of the Weisshorn—A warning—Anecdote of an ascent of the Matterhorn—Imboden sounds the depths of the perfidy of
the human heart—A friendly suggestion—We start for
the Ried Pass—I am accompanied by a guide and
porter of whom I know very little—The ideas of the
ormer become confused—We undertake the guiding—
A dangerous piece of advice—Obliged to resort to
strategy—Fée—Arrangements for ascending the Weisshorn—We set out from Randa—The comforts awaiting
us at the hut—Uncertainty—We start at 4 a.m.—The
delight of climbing a classical peak—The *Arête*—Arrival
on the summit—Descent to Randa—*Après cela, la
déluge.*

"YOU must go up the Weisshorn with me," Imboden had said, as from the summit of the Bieshorn
we admired the beautiful white peak, with its
terraces of broken glacier, and the long and
narrow *arête* of rocks which forms the usual approach to the mountain. And had ever one of

these "palaces of nature" a grander highway by
which to draw near to its solitudes than the narrow
ridge of the Weisshorn, on which the climbers
walk and look down to the broad basin of the
Bies glacier and the hollow between the Weisshorn
and Rothhorn, many thousands of feet below?
Throw a stone from the top of one of those long
snow *couloirs* with which the *arête* is seamed. It
will bound from side to side, adding another to
the many markings in the gulley, and will not stop
till it buries itself far below on the glacier, or
falls into one of the gaping crevasses. Imboden
declared that I should think the passage along the
ridge a most delightful climb, but added, holding
up one of his fingers with a warning gesture, " If
it is in good condition when we ascend it, and
you find it easy, *don't say so*, for numbers of the
people who go up the Weisshorn would find walking
to the Gorner Grat a much more suitable occupa-
tion. We see the folly of that sort of thing too
often on the Matterhorn, and such stupidity will
go on till some one is killed."

He has often amused me by his anecdotes of
people who, while professing to possess much skill

in mountain craft, have to be helped almost as if
they were babes in arms, and he especially mentioned the case of an individual with whom he
made the ascent of the Matterhorn. This person
spent the greater part of the day in telling Imboden
that he knew they would all be killed, and when
they reached the upper hut the traveller offered to
pay the entire tarif (4*l*.) if Imboden would take him
down from there. The latter, however, insisted on
continuing the ascent, while the lion-hearted one,
at every halt, begged with tears in his eyes to be
guided back again to the valley, and offered bribes
which at last accumulated to almost fabulous
sums. Imboden was younger in those days, and
had not sounded to the full the depths of the
perfidy of the human heart. His sensations can
therefore be imagined when, after safely landing
the cringing, terrified, helpless traveller at Zermatt,
he overheard him inform a party of choice spirits,
who were all agape to hear the news, that " The
Matterhorn is a swindle ; there's not a pin to choose
between climbing the Matterhorn and walking
along the high road ! "

Needless to say, Imboden did not disclose the

name of the *intrépide* in question, and such people
are too numerous for the identity of this particular
specimen of the class to be a matter of certainty,
even to those who best know the usual frequenters
of Alpine districts.

Imboden should write a book, and call it,
" Personal recollections of scenes and characters."
There would, I fancy, be some searchings of heart
on its publication; but the work would be interesting in a high degree.

The Weisshorn was a peak which I had long
looked forward to climbing, so I promised Imboden
to telegraph to him from Fée, when my stay there
should have terminated. Meanwhile I prepared to
set out from St. Nicholas by the Ried Pass. As
Imboden was engaged, I took the only man I
could find, and bitterly regretted my bargain. The
guide was quite unknown to me, but I had been
told that he was up to his work, so I thought that
he could probably at least contrive to cross the
Ried. Nevertheless, the excursion was not uneventful, for the individual in question managed
so completely to muddle his brain that, by the time
we had ascended the Balfrinhorn, and stood on the

summit of the pass, he was quite unable to inform us in which direction the descent should be made. The porter was steady and reliable, but, as he had never crossed the pass before, he naturally did not know the route. However, there is not a large choice, and to turn to the right, down the rocks, as soon as the *arête* has been kept to for a short distance, seemed the most natural course to pursue. We therefore carefully descended the wall of rock which overhangs a small glacier, part of which we could see from above. The guide blundered along after us as best he could, continually hooking on the rope to projecting rocks, and, as he was entirely unconscious of this performance, the result was occasionally awkward both to himself and to us.

At last we neared an extremely steep *couloir* of frozen snow, which, about a hundred feet or so lower down the slope, was cut asunder by a gigantic bergschrund. The upper edge of the chasm must have been seventy feet or more above its lower lip, and, to add to the attractions of the place, large stones fell at intervals, and now and then the *couloir* was swept by perfect avalanches of broken fragments of rock. The guide halted in a knowing

manner when he saw this charming spot, and
suggested to us that it would be well to lose no
time in gaining the centre of the *couloir*, as then
we could glissade down it. I alleged my timidity
on steep snow as a reason for not following his
advice, for the man, it was evident, was quite in
earnest. Continuing, therefore, to descend by the
rocks, we gradually drew near to the glacier, from
which, however, we were cut off by a large crevasse.
Catching sight of a bridge by which it could be
crossed, I steered towards it, and had the doubtful
satisfaction of hearing my follower observe that, if
we attempted to cross at that one particular place,
we should all, without doubt, be killed. Indeed, so
tiresome did he become about the matter that I
could only manage him by a most dishonest piece
of strategy. It was evident that any suggestion
coming from me would be doomed, so I sharply
informed him that he was quite mistaken in supposing that I wished to cross the snow bridge, as
my intention was to jump the crevasse from the
place at which we stood. This settled the question.
Assuring me that nothing would induce him to go
over, except by the snow bridge, which was what

he had advocated from the beginning, and that my
plan was, as he had said before, madness, he
straightway turned towards the bridge, and before
long we were able to unrope. Fée was reached by
dinner-time, and the hotel as usual was crowded to
overflowing ; but the landlady had not locked
herself up in the bureau in despair, as I have been
told she has sometimes done, and a room for me
was forthcoming, thanks to some friends who had
secured it the day before.

I spent about a fortnight at Feé, taking photographs and making small excursions. Then the
time drew near when I had to think of leaving, so
taking advantage of Mr. Barnes's offer of Imboden
on an off-day, I telegraphed to Zermatt and appointed the Tuesday following for the Weisshorn.
When ascending the Weissmies on the Saturday
before, I was much disgusted to notice a change
in the weather, and snow beginning to fall during
the descent, I was simply in despair. The next
morning brought a cloudless sky, but the higher
parts of the splendid amphitheatre of peaks round
Fée glittered in garments of fresh snow. I was
sorrowfully trying to resign myself to the idea of

my excursion being postponed till the following season, when a telegram from Mr. Barnes to the effect that "the Weisshorn is believed to be all right," raised me to the seventh heaven.

Hastily packing, I started for St. Nicholas, and the next day, by one o'clock, I was at Randa. There I was greeted by a note which told me that Imboden was engaged on an ascent of the Weisshorn that very day, but that on mounting to the hut with the porter, I should find my guide there. All the provisions had been most thoughtfully ordered, and everything arranged for me by my friend, so very soon the porter and I set out, and began slowly to ascend through the pine-woods. Before long we met Mr. Donkin and Mr. Barnes, who told us that the condition of the Weisshorn was very fair, considering the large amount of fresh snow which had fallen. Then on again till the trees grew stunted and finally ceased altogether and grassy slopes took their place. At last a dilapidated stone hut, built close under the rocks could be seen, and on the roof sat Imboden, while blue smoke curled up from the chimney of the cabin, telling us that we should not have to wait

long before beginning to cook our dinner. The
inside of our lodging was even less inviting than
the exterior, and judging by the amount of daylight which could be seen through various cracks
and holes, it would evidently not be a desirable
residence during a shower of rain. We were soon
installed, and our not very elaborate dinner concluded. The next thing to do was to go out and
examine the weather. I was much annoyed to
see that heavy thunder-clouds covered the sky, and
already a few drops of rain had begun to fall.
Imboden shook his head, and declined to give an
opinion one way or the other, while the porter
loudly bewailed the state of things, and addressed
various uncomplimentary remarks, couched in very
strong language, to the darkening heavens. However, as there was no use in sitting up to contemplate
so unpleasing a sight we retired to our couches of
damp straw. Mr. Barnes had kindly left a large
plaid, and this proved an excellent protection
against the rain which steadily dripped through
the dilapidated roof. There was a hole in the wall
near my corner through which I could see the sky.
Every now and then I glanced out, and towards

midnight a star or two appeared and gave hope of
an improvement in the weather. At two o'clock,
the hour fixed for our rest to terminate, Imboden
still slept. I knew that he must require a good
night after his exertions of the day before, and, as
there was plenty of time, I did not call him till
three. Then the preparations for departure began,
for the sky was once more cloudless and our late
period of uncertainty lent a greater pleasure to the
thought of the enjoyable day in store for us. It
was just four o'clock when we set out. First, slopes
of stones had to be crossed, then some hard snow
which crunched cheerily under our feet, succeeded
by a scramble up a short, steep gully. Here the
lantern was left, and, shortly afterwards, we began
to ascend the broken and easy rocks by which
the beginning of the *arête* is gained. The fresh
snow had filled up all the hollows amongst these
rocks, and the climb was not such a pleasant one
as it generally is. At least, so said Imboden, but
I enjoyed every part of the work that day, and
having heard so much of the Weisshorn, every step
was like renewing an old friendship. I think that
next to ascending a new peak, there is no delight

so great as making the acquaintance of one of the classical giants of the Alps. Every feature is already familiar from the descriptions of the pioneers of mountaineering, and there is a sensation of being thoroughly at home which is intensely pleasant.

As soon as we reached the beginning of the ridge, our first halt was made, and we seated ourselves comfortably amongst the rocks for breakfast. The *arête* looked most inviting, with its gendarmes or rocky towers, some of which have to be climbed over. Breakfast finished, we began the passage of the ridge, and a more enjoyable scramble I never had. The foothold and handhold is so solid that one need never feel insecure, and the view down on both sides is striking in the extreme. "I told you that you would like it," remarked Imboden as he saw how thoroughly I appreciated the climb. The principal gendarme was capped with snow, and, on many of the rocks, there was a covering two or three feet deep, but it was in good condition and did not delay us much. At the end of the ridge there was a narrow *arête* of snow, topped by a cornice, and here it is that travellers unskilled in

mountain climbing are apt to be made uncomfortable by the sight of the valley, as viewed through
a hole in the cornice pierced by an axe or a finger,
and this miniature picture is certainly not reassuring, but the party can keep well down the slope
during most of the time, so that, even if there is a
little difficulty, there is no danger. A short distance
above this part of the mountain we again halted, and
after having had something to eat, left the knapsacks
and pursued our way up the final snow slope. The
steps of the day before had been melted away and
new ones had to be cut. The last few minutes
seemed interminable and I was by no means sorry
when Imboden cried "Here we are!" and I saw
that we had reached the summit.

It was just nine o'clock. Blue sky was still
overhead, but in the valleys white clouds could
be seen, like tufts of eider-down floating towards
the earth. The Visp with its many windings,
and the village of Randa were visible, and far
below broad glaciers swept past our peak, and
rival summits raised their heads from the icy waves
which slowly but ceaselessly moved on around them.
Glancing towards Zinal, the cliffs fell away in

magnificent precipices, appalling to look down.
The actual summit of the Weisshorn terminates in
a sharp point of frozen snow, and the three sides
correspond to the three faces of the mountain.   In
order that the travellers may rest at the top, a
platform must be cut for them.   Along the ridge
which, after descending, rises again to form the
crest of the Bieshorn, huge cornices hung over,
fringed with glittering icicles, which fell off from
time to time and danced gaily down the slope.
We spent one delightful hour in admiring the
lavish display of well-known peaks around us, and
then we began the descent.   Far below the long
arête could be seen, and a vapoury mass hung
against it, and gradually thick mists boiled up on
either side.   The effect of the ridge thus cut off
from the earth was most curious and very beautiful ;
I have never seen anything of the kind more striking.
The fresh snow delayed us a good deal going down,
as it was, by that time, so wet and slippery.   However, by half-past one o'clock we were at the hut,
and, after a short rest there, descended to Randa.
The same afternoon I drove to St. Nicholas.
Next day the sky was obscured by clouds, and,

towards evening, heavy rain fell. But we had been up the Weisshorn and " after that the deluge "—also the dentist at Lucerne. Bad weather was of no consequence during the week of purgatory spent there, and when, every morning, I saw the down-pour still continuing, I congratulated myself on having utilized the last fine day of the season for an excursion the pleasant recollection of which, in a measure, compensated for the miseries I was called upon to endure at the dentist's hands.

CONCLUSION.

Reasons for venturing to present this work to the public, and good wishes for those who visit Switzerland for health or pleasure.

I HAVE not published this little book " in order to supply a long-felt want." On the contrary, I have no reason to suppose that it fills a gap of any sort. I have derived much enjoyment from the labour of writing it, and have felt some of the old pleasure of the excursions come back, as I tried to recall each point of interest, and if I can give the very least amusement to even one of my readers, my task has not been unprofitable. This is really my feeling with regard to it, and if I might suggest a moral to be drawn from some of the incidents related, it would be in no wise to copy the manner in which many of my excursions were made, but to be as prudent with regard to small climbs in winter as if you were setting out for the Dent

Blanche in summer, and on no account to unnecessarily handicap yourself by taking either guides or friends with you about whose climbing powers and endurance you feel any doubt.

I might go prosing and twaddling on for another ten pages, as is not unfrequently the case with "conclusions," but having nothing more to impart to my readers, now that I have said a few words of apology for venturing to present this book to the public, I do not doubt that I shall act wisely in terminating in a more abrupt manner. I will therefore merely wish all those who visit Switzerland for their pleasure as much enjoyment as I have derived from my travels there, and I heartily desire for the invalids who go in search of health and strength, a benefit as great, from the pure, bracing air, as has been obtained by the author of this little work.

LONDON:
PRINTED BY GILBERT AND RIVINGTON, LIMITED,
ST. JOHN'S SQUARE.

A Catalogue of American and Foreign Books Published or Imported by MESSRS. SAMPSON LOW & CO. *can be had on application.*

Crown Buildings, 188, *Fleet Street, London,*
October, 1885.

𝔄 𝔖𝔢𝔩𝔢𝔠𝔱𝔦𝔬𝔫 𝔣𝔯𝔬𝔪 𝔱𝔥𝔢 𝔏𝔦𝔰𝔱 𝔬𝔣 𝔅𝔬𝔬𝔨𝔰

PUBLISHED BY

SAMPSON LOW, MARSTON, SEARLE, & RIVINGTON.

ALPHABETICAL LIST.

ABOUT Some Fellows. By an ETON BOY, Author of "A Day of my Life." Cloth limp, square 16mo, 2s. 6d.

Adams (C. K.) Manual of Historical Literature. Cr. 8vo, 12s. 6d.

Alcott (Louisa M.) Jack and Jill. 16mo, 5s.

——— *Old-Fashioned Thanksgiving Day.* 3s. 6d.

——— *Proverb Stories.* 16mo, 3s. 6d.

——— *Spinning-Wheel Stories.* 16mo, 5s.

——— See also "Rose Library."

Alden (W. L.) Adventures of Jimmy Brown, written by himself. Illustrated. Small crown 8vo, cloth, 2s. 6d.

Aldrich (T. B.) Friar Jerome's Beautiful Book, &c. Very choicely printed on hand-made paper, parchment cover, 3s. 6d.

——— *Poetical Works.* Édition de Luxe. 8vo, 21s.

Alford (Lady Marian) Needlework as Art. With over 100 Woodcuts, Photogravures, &c. Royal 8vo, 42s.; large paper, 84s.

Amateur Angler's Days in Dove Dale : Three Weeks' Holiday in July and August, 1884. By E. M. Printed by Whittingham, at the Chiswick Press. Cloth gilt, 1s. 6d.; fancy boards, 1s.

American Men of Letters. Thoreau, Irving, Webster. 2s. 6d. each.

Anderson (W.) Pictorial Arts of Japan. With 80 full-page and other Plates, 16 of them in Colours. Large imp. 4to, gilt binding, gilt edges, 8l. 8s.; or in four parts, 2l. 2s. each.

Angler's Strange Experiences (An). By COTSWOLD ISYS. With numerous Illustrations, 4to, 5s. New Edition, 3s. 6d.

Angling. See Amateur, "British Fisheries Directory," "Cutcliffe," "Martin," "Stevens," "Theakston," "Walton," and "Wells."

Arnold (Edwin) Birthday Book. 4s. 6d.

A

Biographies of the Great Artists (*continued*) :—

Leonardo da Vinci.
Little Masters of Germany, by W. B. Scott.
Mantegna and Francia.
Meissonier, by J. W. Mollett, 2s. 6d.
Michelangelo Buonarotti, by Clément.
Murillo, by Ellen E. Minor, 2s. 6d.
Overbeck, by J. B. Atkinson.
Raphael, by N. D'Anvers.
Rembrandt, by J. W. Mollett.

Reynolds, by F. S. Pulling.
Rubens, by C. W. Kett.
Tintoretto, by W. R. Osler.
Titian, by R. F. Heath.
Turner, by Cosmo Monkhouse.
Vandyck and Hals, by P. R. Head
Velasquez, by E. Stowe.
Vernet and Delaroche, by J. Rees.
Watteau, by J. W. Mollett, 2s. 6d.
Wilkie, by J. W. Mollett.

Bird (*F. J.*) *American Practical Dyer's Companion.* 8vo, 42s.

Bird (*H. E.*) *Chess Practice.* 8vo, 2s. 6d.

Black (*Wm.*) *Novels.* See " Low's Standard Library."

Blackburn (*Charles F.*) *Hints on Catalogue Titles and Index* Entries, with a Vocabulary of Terms and Abbreviations, chiefly from Foreign Catalogues. Royal 8vo, 14s.

Blackburn (*Henry*) *Breton Folk.* With 171 Illust. by RANDOLPH CALDECOTT. Imperial 8vo, gilt edges, 21s.; plainer binding, 10s. 6d.

—— *Pyrenees* (*The*). With 100 Illustrations by GUSTAVE DORÉ, corrected to 1881. Crown 8vo, 7s. 6d.

Blackmore (*R. D.*) *Lorna Doone.* *Edition de luxe.* Crown 4to, very numerous Illustrations, cloth, gilt edges, 31s. 6d.; parchment, uncut, top gilt, 35s. Cheap Edition, small post 8vo, 6s.

—— *Novels.* See " Low's Standard Library."

Blaikie (*William*) *How to get Strong and how to Stay so.* Rational, Physical, Gymnastic, &c., Exercises. Illust., sm. post 8vo, 5s.

—— *Sound Bodies for our Boys and Girls.* 16mo, 2s. 6d.

Bonwick (*Jos.*) *British Colonies and their Resources.* 1 vol., cloth, 5s. Sewn—I. Asia, 1s.; II. Africa, 1s.; III. America, 1s.; IV. Australasia, 1s.

Bosanquet (*Rev. C.*) *Blossoms from the King's Garden* : Sermons for Children. 2nd Edition, small post 8vo, cloth extra, 6s.

Boussenard (*L.*) *Crusoes of Guiana.* Illustrated. 5s.

—— *Gold-seekers, a Sequel.* Illustrated. 16mo, 5s.

Boy's Froissart. King Arthur. Mabinogion. Percy. See LANIER.

Bradshaw (*J.*) *New Zealand as it is.* 8vo, 12s. 6d.

Brassey (*Lady*) *Tahiti.* With 31 Autotype Illustrations after Photos. by Colonel STUART-WORTLEY. Fcap. 4to, 21s.

Bright (*John*) *Public Letters.* Crown 8vo, 7s. 6d.

Brisse (Baron) Ménus (366). A *ménu*, in French and English, for every Day in the Year. Translated by Mrs. MATTHEW CLARKE. 2nd Edition. Crown 8vo, 5*s.*

British Fisheries Directory, 1883-84. Small 8vo, 2*s. 6d.*

Brittany. See BLACKBURN.

Brown. *Life and Letters of John Brown, Liberator of Kansas,* and Martyr of Virginia. By F. B. SANBORN. Illustrated. 8vo, 12*s. 6d.*

Browne (G. Lennox) Voice Use and Stimulants. Sm. 8vo, 3*s. 6d.*

―――― *and Behnke (Emil) Voice, Song, and Speech.* Illustrated, 3rd Edition, medium 8vo, 15*s.*

Bryant (W. C.) and Gay (S. H.) History of the United States. 4 vols., royal 8vo, profusely Illustrated, 60*s.*

Bryce (Rev. Professor) Manitoba. With Illustrations and Maps. Crown 8vo, 7*s. 6d.*

Bunyan's Pilgrim's Progress. With 138 original Woodcuts. Small post 8vo, cloth gilt, 3*s. 6d.*; gilt edges, 4*s.*

Burnaby (Capt.) On Horseback through Asia Minor. 2 vols., 8vo, 38*s.* Cheaper Edition, 1 vol., crown 8vo, 10*s. 6d.*

Burnaby (Mrs. F.) High Alps in Winter; or, Mountaineering in Search of Health. By Mrs. FRED BURNABY. With Portrait of the Authoress, Map, and other Illustrations. Handsome cloth, 14*s.*

Butler (W. F.) The Great Lone Land; an Account of the Red River Expedition, 1869-70. New Edition, cr. 8vo, cloth extra, 7*s. 6d.*

―――― *Invasion of England, told twenty years after, by an Old* Soldier. Crown 8vo, 2*s. 6d.*

―――― *Red Cloud; or, the Solitary Sioux.* Imperial 16mo, numerous illustrations, gilt edges, 5*s.*

―――― *The Wild North Land; the Story of a Winter Journey* with Dogs across Northern North America. 8vo, 18*s.* Cr. 8vo, 7*s. 6d.*

Buxton (H. J. W.) Painting, English and American. Crown 8vo, 5*s.*

*C*ADOGAN *(Lady A.) Illustrated Games of Patience.* Twenty-four Diagrams in Colours, with Text. Fcap. 4to, 12*s. 6d.*

California. See "Nordhoff."

Cambridge Staircase (A). By the Author of "A Day of my Life at Eton." Small crown 8vo, cloth, 2*s. 6d.*

Cambridge Trifles ; from an Undergraduate Pen. By the Author
of "A Day of my Life at Eton," &c. 16mo, cloth extra, 2s. 6d.

Carleton (Will) Farm Ballads, Farm Festivals, and Farm
Legends. 1 vol., small post 8vo, 3s. 6d.

—— *City Ballads.* With Illustrations. 12s. 6d.

—— See also "Rose Library."

Carnegie (A.) American Four-in-Hand in Britain. Small
4to, Illustrated, 10s. 6d. Popular Edition, 1s.

—— *Round the World.* 8vo, 10s. 6d.

Chairman's Handbook (The). By R. F. D. PALGRAVE, Clerk of
the Table of the House of Commons. 5th Edition, 2s.

Changed Cross (The), and other Religious Poems. 16mo, 2s. 6d.

Charities of London. See Low's.

Chattock (R. S.) Practical Notes on Etching. Sec. Ed., 8vo, 7s. 6d.

Chess. See BIRD (H. E.).

Children's Praises. Hymns for Sunday-Schools and Services.
Compiled by LOUISA H. H. TRISTRAM. 4d.

Choice Editions of Choice Books. 2s. 6d. each. Illustrated by
C. W. COPE, R.A., T. CRESWICK, R.A., E. DUNCAN, BIRKET
FOSTER, J. C. HORSLEY, A.R.A., G. HICKS, R. REDGRAVE, R.A.,
C. STONEHOUSE, F. TAYLER, G. THOMAS, H. J. TOWNSHEND,
E. H. WEHNERT, HARRISON WEIR, &c.

Bloomfield's Farmer's Boy.	Milton's L'Allegro.
Campbell's Pleasures of Hope.	Poetry of Nature. Harrison Weir.
Coleridge's Ancient Mariner.	Rogers' (Sam.) Pleasures of Memory.
Goldsmith's Deserted Village.	Shakespeare's Songs and Sonnets.
Goldsmith's Vicar of Wakefield.	Tennyson's May Queen.
Gray's Elegy in a Churchyard.	Elizabethan Poets.
Keat's Eve of St. Agnes.	Wordsworth's Pastoral Poems.

"Such works are a glorious beatification for a poet."—*Athenæum.*

Christ in Song. By PHILIP SCHAFF. New Ed., gilt edges, 6s.

Chromo-Lithography. See "Audsley."

Collingwood (Harry) Under the Meteor Flag. The Log of a
Midshipman. Illustrated, small post 8vo, gilt, 6s.; plainer, 5s.

—— *The Voyage of the "Aurora."* Illustrated, small post
8vo, gilt, 6s. ; plainer, 5s.

Colvile (H. E.) Accursed Land: Water Way of Edom. 10s. 6d.

Composers. See "Great Musicians."

Confessions of a Frivolous Girl. Cr. 8vo, 6s. Paper boards, 1s.

Cook (Dutton) Book of the Play. New Edition. 1 vol., 3s. 6d.

—— *On the Stage: Studies of Theatrical History and the Actor's Art.* 2 vols., 8vo, cloth, 24s.

Costume. See SMITH (J. MOYR).

Cowen (Jos., M.P.) Life and Speeches. By MAJOR JONES 8vo, 14s.

Curtis (C. B.) Velazquez and Murillo. With Etchings, &c. Royal 8vo, 31s. 6d.; large paper, 63s.

Custer (E. B.) Boots and Saddles. Life in Dakota with General Custer. Crown 8vo, 8s. 6d.

Cutcliffe (H. C.) Trout Fishing in Rapid Streams. Cr. 8vo, 3s. 6d.

D'ANVERS (N.) An Elementary History of Art. Crown 8vo, 10s. 6d.

—— *Elementary History of Music.* Crown 8vo, 2s. 6d.

—— *Handbooks of Elementary Art—Architecture; Sculpture; Old Masters; Modern Painting.* Crown 8vo, 3s. 6d. each.

Davis (C. T.) Manufacture of Bricks, Tiles, Terra-Cotta, &c. Illustrated. 8vo, 25s.

—— *Manufacture of Leather.* With many Illustrations. 52s. 6d.

Dawidowsky (F.) Glue, Gelatine, Isinglass, Cements, &c. 8vo, 12s. 6d.

Day of My Life (A); or, Every-Day Experiences at Eton. By an ETON BOY. 16mo, cloth extra, 2s. 6d.

Day's Collacon: an Encyclopædia of Prose Quotations. Imperial 8vo, cloth, 31s. 6d.

Decoration. Vols. II. to IX. New Series, folio, 7s. 6d. each.

Dogs in Disease: their Management and Treatment. By ASH· MONT. Crown 8vo, 7s. 6d.

Donnelly (Ignatius) Atlantis; or, the Antediluvian World. 7th Edition, crown 8vo, 12s. 6d.

—— *Ragnarok: The Age of Fire and Gravel.* Illustrated, Crown 8vo, 12s. 6d.

Doré (Gustave) Life and Reminiscences. By BLANCHE ROOSE-
VELT. With numerous Illustrations from the Artist's previously un-
published Drawings. Medium 8vo, 24*s.*

Dougall (James Dalziel) Shooting: its Appliances, Practice,
and Purpose. New Edition, revised with additions. Crown 8vo, 7*s.* 6*d.*
"The book is admirable in every way. . . . . We wish it every success."—*Globe.*
"A very complete treatise. . . . . Likely to take high rank as an authority on
shooting."—*Daily News.*

Drama. See COOK (DUTTON).

Dyeing. See BIRD (F. J.).

EDUCATIONAL Works published in Great Britain. A
Classified Catalogue. Second Edition, 8vo, cloth extra, 5*s.*

Egypt. See "De Leon," "Foreign Countries."

Eight Months on the Gran Ciacco of the Argentine Republic.
8vo, 12*s.* 6*d.*

Electricity. See GORDON.

Elliot (Adm. Sir G.) Future Naval Battles, and how to Fight
them. Numerous Illustrations. Royal 8vo, 14*s.*

Emerson (R. W.) Life. By G. W. COOKE. Crown 8vo, 8*s.* 6*d.*

English Catalogue of Books. Vol. III., 1872—1880. Royal
8vo, half-morocco, 42*s.* See also "Index."

English Etchings. A Periodical published Monthly.

English Philosophers. Edited by E. B. IVAN MÜLLER, M.A.

A series intended to give a concise view of the works and lives of English
thinkers. Crown 8vo volumes of 180 or 200 pp., price 3*s.* 6*d.* each.

Francis Bacon, by Thomas Fowler.	*John Stuart Mill, by Miss Helen
Hamilton, by W. H. S. Monck.	Taylor.
Hartley and James Mill, by G. S.	Shaftesbury and Hutcheson, by
Bower.	Professor Fowler.
	Adam Smith, by J. A. Farrer.

* *Not yet published.*

Esmarch (Dr. Friedrich) Treatment of the Wounded in War.
Numerous Coloured Plates and Illust., 8vo, strongly bound, 1*l.* 8*s.*

Etching. See CHATTOCK, and ENGLISH ETCHINGS.

Etchings (Modern) of Celebrated Paintings. 4to, 31*s.* 6*d.*

FARM Ballads, Festivals, and Legends. See "Rose Library."

Fauriel (Claude) Last Days of the Consulate. Cr. 8vo, 10s. 6d.

Fawcett (Edgar) A Gentleman of Leisure. 1s.

Feilden (H. St. C.) Some Public Schools, their Cost and Scholarships. Crown 8vo, 2s. 6d.

Fenn (G. Manville) Off to the Wilds : A Story for Boys. Profusely Illustrated. Crown 8vo, 7s. 6d. ; also 5s.

—— *The Silver Cañon : a Tale of the Western Plains.* Illustrated, small post 8vo, gilt, 6s.; plainer, 5s.

Fennell (Greville) Book of the Roach. New Edition, 12mo, 2s.

Ferns. See HEATH.

Fields (J. T.) Yesterdays with Authors. New Ed., 8vo, 10s. 6d.

Fleming (Sandford) England and Canada : a Summer Tour. Crown 8vo, 6s.

Florence. See "Yriarte."

Folkard (R., Jun.) Plant Lore, Legends, and Lyrics. Illustrated, 8vo, 16s.

*Forbes (H. O.) Naturalist's Wanderings in the Eastern Archi*pelago. Illustrated, 8vo, 21s.

Foreign Countries and British Colonies. A series of Descriptive Handbooks. Crown 8vo, 3s. 6d. each.

Australia, by J. F. Vesey Fitzgerald.
Austria, by D. Kay, F.R.G.S.
*Canada, by W. Fraser Rae.
Denmark and Iceland, by E. C. Otté.
Egypt, by S. Lane Poole, B.A.
France, by Miss M. Roberts.
Germany, by S. Baring-Gould.
Greece, by L. Sergeant, B.A.
*Holland, by R. L. Poole.
Japan, by S. Mossman.
*New Zealand.
*Persia, by Major-Gen. Sir F. Goldsmid.

Peru, by Clements R. Markham, C.B.
Russia, by W. R. Morfill, M.A.
Spain, by Rev. Wentworth Webster.
Sweden and Norway, by F. H. Woods.
*Switzerland, by W. A. P. Coolidge, M.A.
*Turkey-in-Asia, by J. C. McCoan, M.P.
West Indies, by C. H. Eden, F.R.G.S.

* *Not ready yet.*

Frampton (Mary) Journal, Letters, and Anecdotes, 1799—1846. 8vo, 14s.

Franc (Maud Jeanne). The following form one Series, small
post 8vo, in uniform cloth bindings, with gilt edges :—

Emily's Choice. 5s.	Vermont Vale. 5s.
Hall's Vineyard. 4s.	Minnie's Mission. 4s.
John's Wife : A Story of Life in	Little Mercy. 4s.
South Australia. 4s.	Beatrice Melton's Discipline. 4s.
Marian ; or, The Light of Some	No Longer a Child. 4s.
One's Home. 5s.	Golden Gifts. 4s.
Silken Cords and Iron Fetters. 4s.	Two Sides to Every Question. 4s.
Into the Light. 4s.	Master of Ralston, 4s.

Francis (Frances) Elric and Ethel : a Fairy Tale. Illustrated.
Crown 8vo, 3s. 6d.

French. See "Julien."

Froissart. See "Lanier."

GALE (F. ; the Old Buffer) Modern English Sports : their
Use and Abuse. Crown 8vo, 6s. ; a few large paper copies, 10s. 6d.

Garth (Philip) Ballads and Poems from the Pacific. Small post
8vo, 6s.

Gentle Life (Queen Edition). 2 vols. in 1, small 4to, 6s.

THE GENTLE LIFE SERIES.

Price 6s. each ; or in calf extra, price 10s. 6d. ; Smaller Edition, cloth
extra, 2s. 6d., except where price is named.

The Gentle Life. Essays in aid of the Formation of Character
of Gentlemen and Gentlewomen.

About in the World. Essays by Author of "The Gentle Life."

Like unto Christ. A New Translation of Thomas à Kempis'
"De Imitatione Christi."

Familiar Words. An Index Verborum, or Quotation Handbook. 6s.

Essays by Montaigne. Edited and Annotated by the Author
of "The Gentle Life."

The Gentle Life. 2nd Series.

The Silent Hour : Essays, Original and Selected. By the
Author of "The Gentle Life."

Half-Length Portraits. Short Studies of Notable Persons.
By J. HAIN FRISWELL.

Essays on English Writers, for the Self-improvement of Students in English Literature.

Other People's Windows. By J. HAIN FRISWELL. 6s.

A Man's Thoughts. By J. HAIN FRISWELL.

The Countess of Pembroke's Arcadia. By Sir PHILIP SIDNEY. New Edition, 6s.

George Eliot: a Critical Study of her Life. By G. W. COOKE. Crown 8vo, 10s. 6d.

Germany. By S. BARING-GOULD. Crown 8vo, 3s. 6d.

Gilder (W. H.) Ice-Pack and Tundra. An Account of the Search for the "Jeannette." 8vo, 18s.

—— *Schwatka's Search.* Sledging in quest of the Franklin Records. Illustrated, 8vo, 12s. 6d.

Gilpin's Forest Scenery. Edited by F. G. HEATH. Post 8vo, 7s. 6d.

Gisborne (W.) New Zealand Rulers and Statesmen. With Portraits. Crown 8vo,

Gordon (General) Private Diary in China. Edited by S. MOSSMAN. Crown 8vo, 7s. 6d.

Gordon (J. E. H., B.A. Cantab.) Four Lectures on Electric Induction at the Royal Institution, 1878-9. Illust., square 16mo, 3s.

—— *Electric Lighting.* Illustrated, 8vo, 18s.

—— *Physical Treatise on Electricity and Magnetism.* 2nd Edition, enlarged, with coloured, full-page, &c., Illust. 2 vols., 8vo, 42s.

—— *Electricity for Schools.* Illustrated. Crown 8vo, 5s.

Gouffé (Jules) Royal Cookery Book. Translated and adapted for English use by ALPHONSE GOUFFÉ, Head Pastrycook to the Queen. New Edition, with plates in colours, Woodcuts, &c., 8vo, gilt edges, 42s.

—— Domestic Edition, half-bound, 10s. 6d.

Grant (General, U.S.) Personal Memoirs. With numerous Illustrations, Maps, &c. 2 vols., 8vo, 28s.

Great Artists. See "Biographies."

Great Musicians. Edited by F. HUEFFER. A Series of Biographies, crown 8vo, 3*s*. each :—

Bach.	Handel.	Purcell.
*Beethoven.	Haydn.	Rossini.
*Berlioz.	*Marcello.	Schubert.
English Church Composers. By BARETT.	Mendelssohn.	Schumann.
	Mozart.	Richard Wagner.
*Glück.	*Palestrina.	Weber.

* In preparation.

Groves (J. Percy) Charmouth Grange : a Tale of the Seventeenth Century. Illustrated, small post 8vo, gilt, 6*s*.; plainer, 5*s*.

Guizot's History of France. Translated by ROBERT BLACK. Super-royal 8vo, very numerous Full-page and other Illustrations. In 8 vols., cloth extra, gilt, each 24*s*. This work is re-issued in cheaper binding, 8 vols., at 10*s*. 6*d*. each.
"It supplies a want which has long been felt, and ought to be in the hands of all students of history."—*Times.*

——————— *Masson's School Edition.* Abridged from the Translation by Robert Black, with Chronological Index, Historical and Genealogical Tables, &c. By Professor GUSTAVE MASSON, B.A. With 24 full-page Portraits, and other Illustrations. 1 vol., 8vo, 600 pp., 10*s*. 6*d*.

Guizot's History of England. In 3 vols. of about 500 pp. each, containing 60 to 70 full-page and other Illustrations, cloth extra, gilt, 24*s*. each ; re-issue in cheaper binding, 10*s*. 6*d*. each.
"For luxury of typography, plainness of print, and beauty of illustration, these volumes, of which but one has as yet appeared in English, will hold their own against any production of an age so luxurious as our own in everything, typography not excepted."—*Times.*

Guyon (Mde.) Life. By UPHAM. 6th Edition, crown 8vo, 6*s*.

HALFORD (F. M.) Floating Flies, and how to Dress them. Coloured plates. 8vo, 15*s*. ; large paper, 30*s*.

Hall (W. W.) How to Live Long; or, 1408 *Health Maxims,* Physical, Mental, and Moral. 2nd Edition, small post 8vo, 2*s*.

Hamilton (E.) Recollections of Fly-fishing for Salmon, Trout, and Grayling. With their Habits, Haunts, and History. Illustrated, small post 8vo, 6*s*.; large paper (100 numbered copies), 10*s*. 6*d*.

Hands (T.) Numerical Exercises in Chemistry. Cr. 8vo, 2*s*. 6*d*. and 2*s*.; Answers separately, 6*d*.

Hardy (Thomas). See LOW'S STANDARD NOVELS.

Hargreaves (Capt.) Voyage round Great Britain. Illustrated. Crown 8vo, 5*s*.

Harland (Marian) Home Kitchen: a Collection of Practical and Inexpensive Receipts. Crown 8vo, 5*s*.

Harper's Monthly Magazine. Published Monthly. 160 pages, fully Illustrated. 1*s*.

> Vol. I. December, 1880, to May, 1881.
> ,, II. June to November, 1881.
> ,, III. December, 1881, to May, 1882.
> ,, IV. June to November, 1882.
> ,, V. December, 1882, to May, 1883.
> ,, VI. June to November, 1883.
> ,, VII. December, 1883, to May, 1884.
> ,, VIII. June to November, 1884.
> ,, IX. December, 1884, to May, 1885.
> ,, X. June to November, 1885.

Super-royal 8vo, 8*s*. 6*d*. each.

"'Harper's Magazine' is so thickly sown with excellent illustrations that to count them would be a work of time ; not that it is a picture magazine, for the engravings illustrate the text after the manner seen in some of our choicest *éditions de luxe*."—*St. James's Gazette*.

"It is so pretty, so big, and so cheap. . . . An extraordinary shillingsworth—160 large octavo pages, with over a score of articles, and more than three times as many illustrations."—*Edinburgh Daily Review*.

"An amazing shillingsworth . . . combining choice literature of both nations."—*Nonconformist*.

Harper's Young People. Vol. I., profusely Illustrated with woodcuts and 12 coloured plates. Royal 4to, extra binding, 7*s*. 6*d*. ; gilt edges, 8*s*. Published Weekly, in wrapper, 1*d*. 12mo. Annual Subscription, post free, 6*s*. 6*d*. ; Monthly, in wrapper, with coloured plate, 6*d*. ; Annual Subscription, post free, 7*s*. 6*d*.

Harrison (Mary) Skilful Cook: a Practical Manual of Modern Experience. Crown 8vo, 5*s*.

Hatton (F.) North Borneo. With Biographical Sketch by JOS. HATTON. Illustrated from Original Drawings, Map, &c. 8vo, 18*s*.

Hatton (Joseph) Journalistic London: with Engravings and Portraits of Distinguished Writers of the Day. Fcap. 4to, 12*s*. 6*d*.

—— *Three Recruits, and the Girls they left behind them.* Small post 8vo, 6*s*.

> "It hurries us along in unflagging excitement."—*Times*.

Heath (Francis George) Autumnal Leaves. New Edition, with Coloured Plates in Facsimile from Nature. Crown 8vo, 14*s*

—— *Fern Paradise.* New Edition, with Plates and Photos., crown 8vo, 12*s*. 6*d*.

Heath (*Francis George*) *Fern World.* With Nature-printed Coloured Plates. Crown 8vo, gilt edges, 12s. 6d. Cheap Edition, 6s.

————— *Gilpin's Forest Scenery.* Illustrated, 8vo, 12s. 6d.; New Edition, 7s. 6d.

————— *Our Woodland Trees.* With Coloured Plates and Engravings. Small 8vo, 12s. 6d.

————— *Peasant Life in the West of England.* New Edition, crown 8vo, 10s. 6d.

————— *Sylvan Spring.* With Coloured, &c., Illustrations. 12s. 6d.

————— *Trees and Ferns.* Illustrated, crown 8vo, 3s. 6d.

Heldmann (*Bernard*) *Mutiny on Board the Ship "Leander."* Small post 8vo, gilt edges, numerous Illustrations, 5s.

Henty (*G. A.*) *Winning his Spurs.* Illustrations. Cr. 8vo, 5s.

————— *Cornet of Horse : A Story for Boys.* Illust., cr. 8vo, 5s.

————— *Jack Archer : Tale of the Crimea.* Illust., crown 8vo, 5s.

Herrick (*Robert*) *Poetry.* Preface by AUSTIN DOBSON. With numerous Illustrations by E. A. ABBEY. 4to, gilt edges, 42s.

Hill (*Staveley, Q.C., M.P.*) *From Home to Home : Two Long* Vacations at the Foot of the Rocky Mountains. With Wood Engravings and Photogravures. 8vo, 21s.

Hitchman, Public Life of the Right Hon. Benjamin Disraeli, Earl of Beaconsfield. 3rd Edition, with Portrait. Crown 8vo, 3s. 6d.

Holmes (*O. Wendell*) *Poetical Works.* 2 vols., 18mo, exquisitely printed, and chastely bound in limp cloth, gilt tops, 10s. 6d.

Homer. Iliad, done into English Verse. By A. S. WAY. 5s.

Hudson (*W. H.*) *The Purple Land that England Lost.* Travels and Adventures in the Banda-Oriental, South America. 2 vols, crown 8vo, 21s.

Hundred Greatest Men (*The*). 8 portfolios, 21s. each, or 4 vols., half-morocco, gilt edges, 10 guineas. New Ed., 1 vol., royal 8vo, 21s.

Hygiene and Public Health. Edited by A. H. BUCK, M.D. Illustrated. 2 vols., royal 8vo, 42s.

Hymnal Companion of Common Prayer. See BICKERSTETH.

ILLUSTRATED Text-Books of Art-Education. Edited by
EDWARD J. POYNTER, R.A. Each Volume contains numerous Illustrations, and is strongly bound for Students, price 5*s.* Now ready :—

PAINTING.

Classic and Italian. By PERCY
R. HEAD.
German, Flemish, and Dutch.

French and Spanish.
English and American.

ARCHITECTURE.

Classic and Early Christian.
Gothic and Renaissance. By T. ROGER SMITH.

SCULPTURE.

Antique: Egyptian and Greek.

Index to the English Catalogue, Jan., 1874, *to Dec.,* 1880.
Royal 8vo, half-morocco, 18*s.*

Indian Garden Series. See ROBINSON (PHIL.).

Irving (Henry) Impressions of America. By J. HATTON. 2
vols., 21*s.*; New Edition, 1 vol., 6*s.*

Irving (Washington). Complete Library Edition of his Works
in 27 Vols., Copyright, Unabridged, and with the Author's Latest
Revisions, called the "Geoffrey Crayon" Edition, handsomely printed
in large square 8vo, on superfine laid paper. Each volume, of about
500 pages, fully Illustrated. 12*s.* 6*d.* per vol. *See also* "Little Britain."

————————— ("American Men of Letters.") 2*s.* 6*d.*

JAMES (C.) Curiosities of Law and Lawyers. 8vo, 7*s.* 6*d*

Japan. See AUDSLEY.

Jerdon (Gertrude) Key-hole Country. Illustrated. Crown 8vo,
cloth, 5*s.*

Johnston (H. H.) River Congo, from its Mouth to Bolobo.
New Edition, 8vo, 21*s.*

Jones (Major) The Emigrants' Friend. A Complete Guide to
the United States. New Edition. 2*s.* 6*d.*

Joyful Lays. Sunday School Song Book. By LOWRY and
DOANE. Boards, 2*s.*

Julien (F.) English Student's French Examiner. 16mo, 2*s.*

———— *First Lessons in Conversational French Grammar.*
Crown 8vo, 1*s.*

Julien (F.) French at Home and at School. Book I., Accidence, &c. Square crown 8vo, 2s.

———— *Conversational French Reader.* 16mo, cloth, 2s. 6d.

———— *Petites Leçons de Conversation et de Grammaire.* New Edition, 3s.

———— *Phrases of Daily Use.* Limp cloth, 6d.

K͟ELSEY (C. B.) Diseases of the Rectum and Anus. Illustrated. 8vo, 18s.

Kempis (Thomas à) Daily Text-Book. Square 16mo, 2s. 6d.; interleaved as a Birthday Book, 3s. 6d.

Kershaw (S. W.) Protestants from France in their English Home. Crown 8vo, 6s.

Kielland. Skipper Worsé. By the Earl of Ducie. Cr. 8vo, 10s. 6d.

Kingston (W. H. G.) Dick Cheveley. Illustrated, 16mo, gilt edges, 7s. 6d.; plainer binding, plain edges, 5s.

———— *Heir of Kilfinnan.* Uniform, 7s. 6d.; also 5s.

———— *Snow-Shoes and Canoes.* Uniform, 7s. 6d.; also 5s.

———— *Two Supercargoes.* Uniform, 7s. 6d.; also 5s.

———— *With Axe and Rifle.* Uniform, 7s. 6d.; also 5s.

Knight (E. F.) Albania and Montenegro. Illust. 8vo, 12s. 6d.

Knight (E. J.) Cruise of the "Falcon." A Voyage round the World in a 30-Ton Yacht. Illust. New Ed. 2 vols., crown 8vo, 24s.

L͟ANIER (Sidney) Boy's Froissart. Illustrated, crown 8vo, gilt edges, 7s. 6d.

———— *Boy's King Arthur.* Uniform, 7s. 6d.

———— *Boy's Mabinogion; Original Welsh Legends of King Arthur.* Uniform, 7s. 6d.

———— *Boy's Percy: Ballads of Love and Adventure, selected from the "Reliques."* Uniform, 7s. 6d.

Lansdell (H.) Through Siberia. 2 vols., 8vo, 30s.; 1 vol., 10s. 6d.

———— *Russia in Central Asia.* Illustrated. 2 vols, 42s.

Larden (W.) School Course on Heat. Second Edition, Illustrated, crown 8vo, 5s.

Lenormant (F.) Beginnings of History. Crown 8vo, 12s. 6d.

Leonardo da Vinci's Literary Works. Edited by Dr. JEAN PAUL RICHTER. Containing his Writings on Painting, Sculpture, and Architecture, his Philosophical Maxims, Humorous Writings, and Miscellaneous Notes on Personal Events, on his Contemporaries, on Literature, &c. ; published from Manuscripts. 2 vols., imperial 8vo, containing about 200 Drawings in Autotype Reproductions, and numerous other Illustrations. Twelve Guineas.

Library of Religious Poetry. Best Poems of all Ages. Edited by SCHAFF and GILMAN. Royal 8vo, 21s.; re-issue in cheaper binding, 10s. 6d.

Lindsay (W. S.) History of Merchant Shipping. Over 150 Illustrations, Maps, and Charts. In 4 vols., demy 8vo, cloth extra. Vols. 1 and 2, 11s. each ; vols. 3 and 4, 14s. each. 4 vols., 50s.

Little Britain, The Spectre Bridegroom, and *Legend of Sleeepy* Hollow. By WASHINGTON IRVING. An entirely New *Edition de luxe.* Illustrated by 120 very fine Engravings on Wood, by Mr. J. D. COOPER. Designed by Mr. CHARLES O. MURRAY. Re-issue, square crown 8vo, cloth, 6s.

Long (Mrs.) Peace and War in the Transvaal. 12mo, 3s. 6d.

Lowell (J. R.) Life of Nathaniel Hawthorn.

Low (Sampson, Jun.) Sanitary Suggestions. Illustrated, crown 8vo, 2s. 6d.

Low's Standard Library of Travel and Adventure. Crown 8vo, uniform in cloth extra, 7s. 6d., except where price is given.
  1. **The Great Lone Land.** By Major W. F. BUTLER, C.B.
  2. **The Wild North Land.** By Major W. F. BUTLER, C.B.
  3. **How I found Livingstone.** By H. M. STANLEY.
  4. **Through the Dark Continent.** By H. M. STANLEY. 12s. 6d.
  5. **The Threshold of the Unknown Region.** By C. R. MARKHAM. (4th Edition, with Additional Chapters, 10s. 6d.)
  6. **Cruise of the Challenger.** By W. J. J. SPRY, R.N.
  7. **Burnaby's On Horseback through Asia Minor.** 10s. 6d.
  8. **Schweinfurth's Heart of Africa.** 2 vols., 15s.
  9. **Marshall's Through America.**
  10. **Lansdell's Through Siberia.** Illustrated and unabridged 10s. 6d.

Low's Standard Novels. Small post 8vo, cloth extra, **6s. each,**
unless otherwise stated.

A Daughter of Heth. By W. BLACK.
In Silk Attire. By W. BLACK.
Kilmeny. A Novel. By W. BLACK
Lady Silverdale's Sweetheart. By W. BLACK.
Sunrise. By W. BLACK.
Three Feathers. By WILLIAM BLACK.
Alice Lorraine. By R. D. BLACKMORE.
Christowell, a Dartmoor Tale. By R. D. BLACKMORE.
Clara Vaughan. By R. D. BLACKMORE.
Cradock Nowell. By R. D. BLACKMORE.
Cripps the Carrier. By R. D. BLACKMORE.
Erema; or, My Father's Sin. By R. D. BLACKMORE.
Lorna Doone. By R. D. BLACKMORE.
Mary Anerley. By R. D. BLACKMORE.
Tommy Upmore. By R. D. BLACKMORE.
An English Squire. By Miss COLERIDGE.
A Story of the Dragonnades; or, Asylum Christi. By the **Rev.**
    E. GILLIAT, M.A.
A Laodicean. By THOMAS HARDY.
Far from the Madding Crowd. By THOMAS HARDY.
Pair of Blue Eyes. By THOMAS HARDY.
Return of the Native. By THOMAS HARDY.
The Hand of Ethelberta. By THOMAS HARDY.
The Trumpet Major. By THOMAS HARDY.
Two on a Tower. By THOMAS HARDY.
Three Recruits. By JOSEPH HATTON.
A Golden Sorrow. By Mrs. CASHEL HOEY. New Edition.
Out of Court. By Mrs. CASHEL HOEY.
Adela Cathcart. By GEORGE MAC DONALD.
Guild Court. By GEORGE MAC DONALD.
Mary Marston. By GEORGE MAC DONALD.
Stephen Archer. New Ed. of "Gifts." By GEORGE MAC DONALD.
The Vicar's Daughter. By GEORGE MAC DONALD.
Weighed and Wanting. By GEORGE MAC DONALD.
Diane. By Mrs. MACQUOID.
Elinor Dryden. By Mrs. MACQUOID.
My Lady Greensleeves. By HELEN MATHERS.
Alaric Spenceley. By Mrs. J. H. RIDDELL.
Daisies and Buttercups. By Mrs. J. H. RIDDELL.
The Senior Partner. By Mrs. J. H. RIDDELL.
A Struggle for Fame. By Mrs. J. H. RIDDELL.
Jack's Courtship. By W. CLARK RUSSELL.
John Holdsworth. By W. CLARK RUSSELL.
A Sailor's Sweetheart. By W. CLARK RUSSELL.
Sea Queen. By W. CLARK RUSSELL.
Watch Below. By W. CLARK RUSSELL.
Wreck of the Grosvenor. By W. CLARK RUSSELL.

Low's Standard Novels—continued.
The Lady Maud. By W. CLARK RUSSELL.
Little Loo. By W. CLARK RUSSELL.
My Wife and I. By Mrs. BEECHER STOWE.
Poganuc People, their Loves and Lives. By Mrs. B. STOWE.
Ben Hur: a Tale of the Christ. By LEW. WALLACE.
Anne. By CONSTANCE FENIMORE WOOLSON.
For the Major. By CONSTANCE FENIMORE WOOLSON. 5*s.*
French Heiress in her own Chateau.

Low's Handbook to the Charities of London. Edited and revised to date by C. MACKESON, F.S.S., Editor of "A Guide to the Churches of London and its Suburbs," &c. Yearly, 1*s.* 6*d.*; Paper, 1*s.*

Lyne (Charles) New Guinea. Illustrated, crown 8vo, 10*s.* 6*d.* An Account of the Establishment of the British Protectorate over the Southern Shores of New Guinea.

M^cCORMICK (R.). Voyages of Discovery in the Arctic and Antarctic Seas in the "Erebus" and "Terror," in Search of Sir John Franklin, &c., with Autobiographical Notice by the Author, who was Medical Officer to each Expedition. With Maps and Lithographic, &c., Illustrations. 2 vols., royal 8vo, 52*s.* 6*d.*

MacDonald (G.) Orts. Small post 8vo, 6*s.*

——— See also " Low's Standard Novels."

Macgregor (John) "Rob Roy" on the Baltic. 3rd Edition, small post 8vo, 2*s.* 6*d.*; cloth, gilt edges, 3*s.* 6*d.*

——— *A Thousand Miles in the "Rob Roy" Canoe.* 11th Edition, small post 8vo, 2*s.* 6*d.*; cloth, gilt edges, 3*s.* 6*d.*

——— *Voyage Alone in the Yawl " Rob Roy."* New Edition, with additions, small post 8vo, 5*s.*; 3*s.* 6*d.* and 2*s.* 6*d.*

Macquoid (Mrs.). See Low's STANDARD NOVELS.

Magazine. See DECORATION, ENGLISH ETCHINGS, HARPER.

Maginn (W.) Miscellanies. Prose and Verse. With Memoir. 2 vols., crown 8vo, 24*s.*

Manitoba. See BRYCE.

Manning (E. F.) Delightful Thames. Illustrated. 4to, fancy boards, 5*s.*

Markham (C. R.) The Threshold of the Unknown Region. Crown 8vo, with Four Maps. 4th Edition. Cloth extra, 10*s.* 6*d.*

——— *War between Peru and Chili*, 1879-1881. Third Ed. Crown 8vo, with Maps, 10*s.* 6*d.*

——— See also "Foreign Countries."

Marshall (W. G.) Through America. New Ed., cr. 8vo, 7*s.* 6*d.*

Martin (F. W.) Float Fishing and Spinning in the Nottingham Style. New Edition. Crown 8vo, 2*s.* 6*d.*

Maury (Commander) Physical Geography of the Sea, and its Meteorology. New Edition, with Charts and Diagrams, cr. 8vo, 6*s.*

Men of Mark: a Gallery of Contemporary Portraits of the most Eminent Men of the Day, specially taken from Life. Complete in Seven Vols., 4to, handsomely bound, cloth, gilt edges, 25*s.* each.

Mendelssohn Family (The), 1729—1847. From Letters and Journals. Translated. New Edition, 2 vols., 8vo, 30*s.*

Mendelssohn. See also "Great Musicians."

Merrifield's Nautical Astronomy. Crown 8vo, 7*s.* 6*d.*

Millard (H. B.) Bright's Disease of the Kidneys. Illustrated. 8vo, 12*s.* 6*d.*

Mitchell (D. G.; Ik. Marvel) Works. Uniform Edition, small 8vo, 5*s.* each.

Bound together.	Reveries of a Bachelor.
Doctor Johns.	Seven Stories, Basement and Attic.
Dream Life.	Wet Days at Edgewood.
Out-of-Town Places.	

Mitford (Mary Russell) Our Village. With 12 full-page and 157 smaller Cuts. Cr. 4to, cloth, gilt edges, 21*s.*; cheaper binding, 10*s.* 6*d.*

Mollett (J. W.) Illustrated Dictionary of Words used in Art and Archæology. Terms in Architecture, Arms, Bronzes, Christian Art, Colour, Costume, Decoration, Devices, Emblems, Heraldry, Lace, Personal Ornaments, Pottery, Painting, Sculpture, &c. Small 4to, 15*s.*

Morley (H.) English Literature in the Reign of Victoria. 2000th volume of the Tauchnitz Collection of Authors. 18mo, 2*s.* 6*d.*

Morwood (V. S.) Our Gipsies in City, Tent, and Van. 8vo, 18*s.*

Muller (E.) Noble Words and Noble Deeds. By PHILIPPOTEAUX. Square imperial 16mo, cloth extra, 7*s.* 6*d.*; plainer binding, 5*s.*

Music. See "Great Musicians."

NEW Zealand. See BRADSHAW.

New Zealand Rulers and Statesmen. See GISBORNE.

Newbiggin's Sketches and Tales. 18mo, 4s.

Nicholls (J. H. Kerry) The King Country: Explorations in New Zealand. Many Illustrations and Map. New Edition, 8vo, 21s.

Nicholson (C.) Work and Workers of the British Association. 12mo, 1s.

Nixon (J.) Complete Story of the Transvaal. 8vo, 12s. 6d.

Nordhoff (C.) California, for Health, Pleasure, and Residence. New Edition, 8vo, with Maps and Illustrations, 12s. 6d.

Northbrook Gallery. Edited by Lord Ronald Gower. 36 Permanent Photographs. Imperial 4to, 63s.; large paper, 105s.

Nursery Playmates (Prince of). 217 Coloured Pictures for Children by eminent Artists. Folio, in coloured boards, 6s.

O'BRIEN (R. B.) Fifty Years of Concessions to Ireland. With a Portrait of T. Drummond. Vol. I., 16s.; II., 16s.

Orvis (C. F.) Fishing with the Fly. Illustrated. 8vo, 12s. 6d.

Our Little Ones in Heaven. Edited by the Rev. H. ROBBINS. With Frontispiece after Sir JOSHUA REYNOLDS. New Edition, 5s.

Owen (Douglas) Marine Insurance Notes and Clauses. New Edition, 14s.

PALLISER (Mrs.) A History of Lace. New Edition, with additional cuts and text. 8vo, 21s.

—— *The China Collector's Pocket Companion.* With upwards of 1000 Illustrations of Marks and Monograms. Small 8vo, 5s.

Pascoe (C. E.) London of To-Day. Illust., crown 8vo, 3s. 6d.

Pharmacopœia of the United States of America. 8vo, 21s.

Philpot (H. J.) Diabetes Mellitus. Crown 8vo, 5s.

—— *Diet System.* Three Tables, in cases, 1s. each.

Pinto (Major Serpa) How I Crossed Africa. With 24 full-page and 118 half-page and smaller Illustrations, 13 small Maps, and 1 large one. 2 vols., 8vo, 42*s*.

Plunkett (Major G. F.) Primer of Orthographic Projection. Elementary Practical Solid Geometry clearly explained. With Problems and Exercises. Specially adapted for Science and Art Classes, and for Students who have not the aid of a Teacher.

Poe (E. A.) The Raven. Illustr. by DORÉ. Imperial folio, 63*s*.

Poems of the Inner Life. Chiefly from Modern Authors. Small 8vo, 5*s*.

Polar Expeditions. See GILDER, MARKHAM, MCCORMICK.

Porter (Noah) Elements of Moral Science. 10*s*. 6*d*.

Powell (W.) Wanderings in a Wild Country; or, Three Years among the Cannibals of New Britain. Illustr., 8vo, 18*s*.; cr. 8vo, 5*s*.

Power (Frank) Letters from Khartoum during the Siege. Fcap. 8vo, boards, 1*s*.

Poynter (Edward J., R.A.). See " Illustrated Text-books."

Publishers' Circular (The), and General Record of British and Foreign Literature. Published on the 1st and 15th of every Month, 3*d*.

REBER (F.) History of Ancient Art. 8vo, 18*s*.

Redford (G.) Ancient Sculpture. Crown 8vo, 5*s*.

Richter (Dr. Jean Paul) Italian Art in the National Gallery. 4to. Illustrated. Cloth gilt, 2*l*. 2*s*.; half-morocco, uncut, 2*l*. 12*s*. 6*d*.

—— See also LEONARDO DA VINCI.

Riddell (Mrs. J. H.) See LOW'S STANDARD NOVELS.

Robin Hood; Merry Adventures of. Written and illustrated by HOWARD PYLE. Imperial 8vo, 15*s*.

Robinson (Phil.) In my Indian Garden. Crown 8vo, limp cloth, 3*s*. 6*d*.

Robinson (Phil.) Indian Garden Series. 1s 6d. ; boards, 1s. each.
I. Chasing a Fortune, &c. : Stories. II. Tigers at Large.

—— *Noah's Ark. A Contribution to the Study of Unnatural* History. Small post 8vo, 12s. 6d.

—— *Sinners and Saints : a Tour across the United States of* America, and Round them. Crown 8vo, 10s. 6d.

—— *Under the Punkah.* Crown 8vo, limp cloth, 5s.

Rockstro (W. S.) History of Music.

Rodrigues (J. C.) The Panama Canal. Crown 8vo, cloth extra, 5s.
"A series of remarkable articles . . . a mine of valuable data for editors and diplomatists."—*New York Nation.*

Roland ; the Story of. Crown 8vo, illustrated, 6s.

Rose (F.) Complete Practical Machinist. New Ed., 12mo, 12s. 6d.

—— *Mechanical Drawing.* ⌐ Illustrated, small 4to, 16s.

Rose Library (The). Popular Literature of all Countries. Each volume, 1s.; cloth, 2s. 6d. Many of the Volumes are Illustrated—
Little Women. By LOUISA M. ALCOTT.

Little Women Wedded. Forming a Sequel to "Little Women."

Little Women and Little Women Wedded. 1 vol., cloth gilt, 3s. 6d.

Little Men. By L. M. ALCOTT. 2s.; cloth gilt, 3s. 6d.

An Old-Fashioned Girl. By LOUISA M. ALCOTT. 2s.; cloth, 3s. 6d.

Work. A Story of Experience. By L. M. ALCOTT. 3s. 6d. ; 2 vols. 1s. each.

Stowe (Mrs. H. B.) The Pearl of Orr's Island.

—— **The Minister's Wooing.**

—— **We and our Neighbours.** 2s.; cloth gilt, 6s.

—— **My Wife and I.** 2s.; cloth gilt, 6s.

Hans Brinker ; or, the Silver Skates. By Mrs. DODGE.

My Study Windows. By J. R. LOWELL.

The Guardian Angel. By OLIVER WENDELL HOLMES.

My Summer in a Garden. By C. D. WARNER.

Dred. By Mrs. BEECHER STOWE. 2s.; cloth gilt, 3s. 6d.

Farm Ballads. By WILL CARLETON.

Farm Festivals. By WILL CARLETON.

Rose Library (The)—continued.

Farm Legends. By WILL CARLETON.

The Clients of Dr. Bernagius. 3s. 6d. ; 2 parts, 1s. each.

The Undiscovered Country. By W. D. HOWELLS. 3s. 6d. and 1s.

Baby Rue. By C. M. CLAY. 3s. 6d. and 1s.

The Rose in Bloom. By L. M. ALCOTT. 2s. ; cloth gilt, 3s. 6d.

Eight Cousins. By L. M. ALCOTT. 2s. ; cloth gilt, 3s. 6d.

Under the Lilacs. By L. M. ALCOTT. 2s. ; also 3s. 6d.

Silver Pitchers. By LOUISA M. ALCOTT. 3s. 6d. and 1s.

Jimmy's Cruise in the "Pinafore," and other Tales. By LOUISA M. ALCOTT. 2s.; cloth gilt, 3s. 6d.

Jack and Jill. By LOUISA M. ALCOTT. 5s.; 2s.

Hitherto. By the Author of the "Gayworthys." 2 vols., 1s. each; 1 vol., cloth gilt, 3s. 6d.

Friends: a Duet. By E. STUART PHELPS. 3s. 6d.

A Gentleman of Leisure. A Novel. By EDGAR FAWCETT. 3s. 6d. ; 1s.

The Story of Helen Troy. 3s. 6d. ; also 1s.

Ross (Mars ; and Stonehewer Cooper) Highlands of Cantabria ; or, Three Days from England. Illustrations and Map, 8vo, 21s.

Round the Yule Log : Norwegian Folk and Fairy Tales. Translated from the Norwegian of P. CHR. ASBJÖRNSEN. With 100 Illustrations after drawings by Norwegian Artists, and an Introduction by E. W Gosse. Impl. 16mo, cloth extra, gilt edges, 7s. 6d. and 5s.

Rousselet (Louis) Son of the Constable of France. Small post 8vo, numerous Illustrations, 5s.

—— *King of the Tigers : a Story of Central India.* Illustrated. Small post 8vo, gilt, 6s.; plainer, 5s.

—— *Drummer Boy.* Illustrated. Small post 8vo, 5s.

Rowbotham (F.) Trip to Prairie Land. The Shady Side of Emigration. 5s.

Russell (W. Clark) English Channel Ports and the Estate of the East and West India Dock Company. Crown 8vo, 1s.

—— *Jack's Courtship.* 3 vols., 31s. 6d. ; 1 vol., 6s.

Russell (W. Clark) The Lady Maud. 3 vols., 31*s.* 6*d.*; 1 vol., 6*s.*

—— *Little Loo.* New Edition, small post 8vo, 6*s.*

—— *My Watch Below; or, Yarns Spun when off Duty.* Small post 8vo, 6*s.*

—— *Sailor's Language.* Illustrated. Crown 8vo, 3*s.* 6*d.*

—— *Sea Queen.* 3 vols., 31*s.* 6*d.*; 1 vol., 6*s.*

—— *Strange Voyage.* Nautical Novel. 3 vols., crown 8vo, 31*s.* 6*d.*

—— *Wreck of the Grosvenor.* 4to, sewed, 6*d.*

—— See also LOW'S STANDARD NOVELS.

SAINTS and their Symbols: A Companion in the Churches and Picture Galleries of Europe. Illustrated. Royal 16mo, 3*s.* 6*d.*

Salisbury (Lord) Life and Speeches. By F. S. Pulling, M.A. With Photogravure Portrait of Lord Salisbury. 2 vols., crown 8vo, 21*s.*

Saunders (A.) Our Domestic Birds: Poultry in England and New Zealand. Crown 8vo, 6*s.*

Scherr (Prof. J.) History of English Literature. Cr. 8vo, 8*s.* 6*d.*

Schley. Rescue of Greely. Maps and Illustrations, 8vo, 12*s.* 6*d.*

Schuyler (Eugène). The Life of Peter the Great. By EUGÈNE SCHUYLER, Author of "Turkestan." 2 vols., 8vo, 32*s.*

Schweinfurth (Georg) Heart of Africa. Three Years' Travels and Adventures in the Unexplored Regions of Central Africa, from 1868 to 1871. Illustrations and large Map. 2 vols., crown 8vo, 15*s.*

Scott (Leader) Renaissance of Art in Italy. 4to, 31*s.* 6*d.*

Sea, River, and Creek. By GARBOARD STREYKE. *The Eastern* Coast. 12mo, 1*s.*

Senior (W.) Waterside Sketches. Imp. 32mo, 1*s.*6*d.*, boards, 1*s.*

Shadbolt and Mackinnon's South African Campaign, 1879. Containing a portrait and biography of every officer who lost his life. 4to, handsomely bound, 2*l.* 10*s.*

Shadbolt (S. H.) Afghan Campaigns of 1878—1880. By
SYDNEY SHADBOLT.   2 vols., royal quarto, cloth extra, 3*l.*

Shakespeare.   Edited by R. GRANT WHITE.   3 vols., crown
8vo, gilt top, 36*s.*; *édition de luxe*, 6 vols., 8vo, cloth extra, 63*s.*

Shakespeare.   See also WHITE (R. GRANT).

"*Shooting Niagara;*" *or, The Last Days of Caucusia.*   By the
Author of "The New Democracy."   Small post 8vo, boards, 1*s.*

Sidney (Sir Philip) Arcadia.   New Edition, 6*s.*

Siegfried : The Story of.   Illustrated, crown 8vo, cloth, 6*s.*

Sinclair (Mrs.) Indigenous Flowers of the Hawaiian Islands.
44 Plates in Colour.   Imp. folio, extra binding, gilt edges, 31*s.* 6*d.*

Sir Roger de Coverley.   Re-imprinted from the "Spectator."
With 125 Woodcuts and special steel Frontispiece.   Small fcap. 4to, 6*s.*

Smith (G.) Assyrian Explorations and Discoveries.   Illustrated
by Photographs and Woodcuts.   New Edition, demy 8vo, 18*s.*

——— *The Chaldean Account of Genesis.*   With many Illustrations.   16*s.*   New Edition, revised and re-written by PROFESSOR
SAYCE, Queen's College, Oxford.   8vo, 18*s.*

Smith (J. Moyr) Ancient Greek Female Costume.   112 full-
page Plates and other Illustrations.   Crown 8vo, 7*s.* 6*d.*

——— *Hades of Ardenne : a Visit to the Caves of Han.*   Crown
8vo, Illustrated, 5*s.*

——— *Legendary Studies, and other Sketches for Decorative*
Figure Panels.   7*s.* 6*d.*

——— *Wooing of Æthra.*   Illustrated.   32mo, 1*s.*

Smith (Sydney) Life and Times.   By STUART J. REID.   Illustrated.   8vo, 21*s.*

Smith (T. Roger) Architecture, Gothic and Renaissance.   Illustrated, crown 8vo, 5*s.*

——————————————— *Classic and Early Christian.*
Illustrated.   Crown 8vo, 5*s.*

Smith (W. R.) Laws concerning Public Health.   8vo, 31*s.* 6*d.*

Somerset (Lady H.) Our Village Life. Words and Illustrations. Thirty Coloured Plates, royal 4to, fancy covers, 5*s.*

Spanish and French Artists. By GERARD SMITH. (Poynter's Art Text-books.) 5*s.*

Spiers' French Dictionary. 29th Edition, remodelled. 2 vols., 8vo, 18*s.*; half bound, 21*s.*

Spry (W. J. J., R.N.) Cruise of H.M.S. " Challenger." With many Illustrations. 6th Edition, 8vo, cloth, 18*s.* Cheap Edition, crown 8vo, 7*s.* 6*d.*

Spyri (Joh.) Heidi's Early Experiences : a Story for Children and those who love Children. Illustrated, small post 8vo, 4*s.* 6*d.*

—————— *Heidi's Further Experiences.* Illust., sm. post 8vo, 4*s.* 6*d.*

Stanley (H. M.) Congo, and Founding its Free State. Illustrated, 2 vols., 8vo, 42*s.*

—————— *How I Found Livingstone.* 8vo, 10*s.* 6*d.* ; cr. 8vo, 7*s.* 6*d.*

—————— *Through the Dark Continent.* Crown 8vo, 12*s.* 6*d.*

Stenhouse (Mrs.) An Englishwoman in Utah. Crown 8vo, 2*s.* 6*d.*

Stevens (E. W.) Fly-Fishing in Maine Lakes. 8*s.* 6*d.*

Stockton (Frank R.) The Story of Viteau. With 16 page Illustrations. Crown 8vo, 5*s.*

Stoker (Bram) Under the Sunset. Crown 8vo, 6*s.*

Stowe (Mrs. Beecher) Dred. Cloth, gilt edges, 3*s.* 6*d.*; boards, 2*s.*

—————— *Little Foxes.* Cheap Ed., 1*s.*; Library Edition, 4*s.* 6*d.*

—————— *My Wife and I.* Small post 8vo, 6*s.*

—————— *Old Town Folk.* 6*s.*; Cheap Edition, 3*s.*

—————— *Old Town Fireside Stories.* Cloth extra, 3*s.* 6*d.*

—————— *We and our Neighbours.* Small post 8vo, 6*s.*

—————— *Poganuc People: their Loves and Lives.* Crown 8vo, 6*s.*

—————— *Chimney Corner.* 1*s.*; cloth, 1*s.* 6*d.*

—————— See also ROSE LIBRARY.

Sullivan (A. M.) Nutshell History of Ireland. Paper boards, 6d.

Sutton (A. K.) A B C Digest of the Bankruptcy Law. 8vo, 3s. and 2s. 6d.

TAINE (H. A.) "Les Origines de la France Contemporaine." Translated by JOHN DURAND.
    I.   **The Ancient Regime.** Demy 8vo, cloth, 16s.
    II.   **The French Revolution.** Vol. 1.   do.
    III.   **Do.**   do.   Vol. 2.   do.
    IV.   **Do.**   do.   Vol. 3.   do.

Talbot (Hon. E.) A Letter on Emigration. 1s.

Tauchnitz's English Editions of German Authors. Each volume, cloth flexible, 2s. ; or sewed, 1s. 6d. (Catalogues post free.)

Tauchnitz (B.) German and English Dictionary. 2s.; paper, 1s. 6d. ; roan, 2s. 6d.

—— *French and English Dictionary.* 2s.; paper, 1s. 6d. ; roan, 2s. 6d.

—— *Italian and English Dictionary.* 2s. ; paper, 1s. 6d. ; roan, 2s. 6d.

—— *Spanish and English.* 2s. ; paper, 1s. 6d. ; roan, 2s. 6d.

Taylor (IV. M.) Paul the Missionary. Crown 8vo, 7s. 6d.

Thausing (Prof) Malt and the Fabrication of Beer. 8vo, 45s.

Theakston (M.) British Angling Flies. Illustrated. Cr. 8vo, 5s.

Thomson (IV.) Algebra for Colleges and Schools. With numerous Examples. 8vo, 5s., Key, 1s. 6x.

Thomson (Jos.) Through Masai Land. Illustrations and Maps. 21s.

Thoreau. American Men of Letters. Crown 8vo, 2s. 6d.

Tolhausen (Alexandre) Grand Supplément du Dictionnaire Technologique. 3s. 6d.

Tristram (Rev. Canon) Pathways of Palestine : A Descriptive Tour through the Holy Land. First Series. Illustrated by 44 Permanent Photographs. 2 vols., folio, cloth extra, gilt edges, 31s. 6d. each.

Trollope (Anthony) Thompson Hall. 1s.

Tromholt (S.) Under the Rays of the Aurora Borealis. By C. SIEWERS. Photographs and Portraits. 2 vols., 8vo, 30s.

Tunis. See REID.

Turner (Edward) Studies in Russian Literature. Cr. 8vo, 8s. 6d.

UNION Jack (The). Every Boy's Paper. Edited by G. A. HENTY. Profusely Illustrated with Coloured and other Plates. Vol. I., 6s. Vols. II., III., IV., 7s. 6d. each.

VASILI (Count) Berlin Society. Translated. Cown 8vo, 6s.

―――― *World of London (La Société de Londres).* Translated. Crown 8vo, 6s.

Velazquez and Murillo. By C. B. CURTIS. With Original Etchings. Royal 8vo, 31s. 6d.; large paper, 63s.

Victoria (Queen) Life of. By GRACE GREENWOOD. With numerous Illustrations. Small post 8vo, 6s.

Vincent (Mrs. Howard) Forty Thousand Miles over Land and Water. With Illustrations engraved under the direction of Mr. H. BLACKBURN. 2 vols, crown 8vo, 21s.

Viollet-le-Duc (E.) Lectures on Architecture. Translated by BENJAMIN BUCKNALL, Architect. With 33 Steel Plates and 200 Wood Engravings. Super-royal 8vo, leather back, gilt top, 2 vols., 3l. 3s.

Vivian (A. P.) Wanderings in the Western Land. 3rd Ed., 10s. 6d.

BOOKS BY JULES VERNE.

LARGE CROWN 8vo. WORKS.	Containing 350 to 600 pp. and from 50 to 100 full-page illustrations.		Containing the whole of the text with some illustrations.	
	In very handsome cloth binding, gilt edges.	In plainer binding, plain edges.	In cloth binding, gilt edges, smaller type.	Coloured boards.
	s. d.	s. d.	s. d.	
20,000 Leagues under the Sea. Parts I. and II..	10 6	5 0	3 6	2 vols., 1s. each.
Hector Servadac	10 6	5 0	3 6	2 vols., 1s. each.
The Fur Country	10 6	5 0	3 6	2 vols., 1s. each.
The Earth to the Moon and a Trip round it	10 6	5 0	{ 2 vols., 2s. ea. }	2 vols., 1s. each.
Michael Strogoff	10 6	5 0	3 6	2 vols., 1s. each.
Dick Sands, the Boy Captain	10 6	5 0	3 6	2 vols., 1s. each.
Five Weeks in a Balloon	7 6	3 6	2 0	1s. 0d.
Adventures of Three Englishmen and Three Russians	7 6	3 6	2 0	1 0
Round the World in Eighty Days	7 6	3 6	2 0	1 0
A Floating City	7 6	3 6	{ 2 0	1 0
The Blockade Runners			2 0	1 0
Dr. Ox's Experiment	—	—	2 0	1 0
A Winter amid the Ice	—	—	2 0	1 0
Survivors of the "Chancellor"	7 6	3 6	{ 2 0	2 vols., 1s. each.
Martin Paz			2 0	1s. 0d.
The Mysterious Island, 3 vols.:—	22 6	10 6	6 0	3 0
I. Dropped from the Clouds	7 6	3 6	2 0	1 0
II. Abandoned	7 6	3 6	2 0	1 0
III. Secret of the Island	7 6	3 6	2 0	1 0
The Child of the Cavern	7 6	3 6	2 0	1 0
The Begum's Fortune	7 6	3 6	2 0	1 0
The Tribulations of a Chinaman	7 6	3 6	2 0	1 0
The Steam House, 2 vols.:—				
I. Demon of Cawnpore	7 6	3 6	2 0	1 0
II. Tigers and Traitors	7 6	3 6	2 0	1 0
The Giant Raft, 2 vols.:—				
I. 800 Leagues on the Amazon	7 6	3 6	2 0	1 0
II. The Cryptogram	7 6	3 6	2 0	1 0
The Green Ray	6 0	5 0	—	1 0
Godfrey Morgan	7 6	3 6	2 0	1 0
Kéraban the Inflexible:—				
I. Captain of the "Guidara"	7 6			
II. Scarpante the Spy	7 6			
The Archipelago on Fire	7 6			
The Vanished Diamond	7 6			
Mathias Sandorf	10 6			

CELEBRATED TRAVELS AND TRAVELLERS. 3 vols. 8vo, 600 pp., 100 full-page illustrations, 12s. 6d.; gilt edges, 14s. each:—(1) THE EXPLORATION OF THE WORLD. (2) THE GREAT NAVIGATORS OF THE EIGHTEENTH CENTURY. (3) THE GREAT EXPLORERS OF THE NINETEENTH CENTURY.

WAHL (W. H.) Galvanoplastic Manipulation for the Electro-Plater. 8vo, 35*s.*

Wallace (L.) Ben Hur: A Tale of the Christ. Crown 8vo, 6*s.*

Waller (Rev. C. H.) The Names on the Gates of Pearl, and other Studies. New Edition. Crown 8vo, cloth extra, 3*s.* 6*d.*

—— *A Grammar and Analytical Vocabulary of the Words in* the Greek Testament. Compiled from Brüder's Concordance. For the use of Divinity Students and Greek Testament Classes. Part I. Grammar. Small post 8vo, cloth, 2*s.* 6*d.* Part II. Vocabulary, 2*s.* 6*d.*

—— *Adoption and the Covenant.* Some Thoughts on Confirmation. Super-royal 16mo, cloth limp, 2*s.* 6*d.*

—— *Silver Sockets; and other Shadows of Redemption.* Sermons at Christ Church, Hampstead. Small post 8vo, 6*s.*

Walton (Iz.) Wallet Book, CIƆIƆLXXXV. 21*s.*; l. p. 42*s.*

Walton (T. H.) Coal Mining. With Illustrations. 4to, 25*s.*

Warder (G. W.) Utopian Dreams and Lotus Leaves. Crown 8vo, 6*s.*

Warner (C. D.) My Summer in a Garden. Boards, 1*s.*; leatherette, 1*s.* 6*d.*; cloth, 2*s.*

Warren (W. F.) Paradise Found; the North Pole the Cradle of the Human Race. Illustrated. Crown 8vo, 12*s.* 6*d.*

Washington Irving's Little Britain. Square crown 8vo, 6*s.*

Watson (P. B.) Marcus Aurelius Antoninus. Portr. 8vo, 15*s*

Webster. (American Men of Letters.) 18mo, 2*s.* 6*d.*

Weir (Harrison) Animal Stories, Old and New, told in Pic- tures and Prose. Coloured, &c., Illustrations. 56 pp., 4to, 5*s.*

Wells (H. P.) Fly Rods and Fly Tackle. Illustrated. 10*s.* 6*d.*

Wheatley (H. B.) and Delamotte (P. H.) Art Work in Porce- lain. Large 8vo, 2*s.* 6*d.*

—— *Art Work in Gold and Silver. Modern.* Large 8vo, 2*s.* 6*d.*

—— *Handbook of Decorative Art.* 10*s.* 6*d.*

Whisperings. Poems. Small post 8vo, cloth extra, gilt edges, 3*s.* 6*d.*

White (R. Grant) England Without and Within. Crown 8vo, 10*s.* 6*d.*

—— *Every-day English.* Crown 8vo, 10*s.* 6*d.*

—— *Studies in Shakespeare.* Crown 8vo, 10*s.* 6*d.*

White (R. Grant) Fate of Mansfield Humphreys, the Episode of Mr. Washington Adams in England, an Apology, &c. Crown 8vo, 6s.

—— *Words and their uses.* New Edit., crown 8vo, 10s. 6d.

Whittier (J. G.) The King's Missive, and later Poems. 18mo, choice parchment cover, 3s. 6d.

—— *The Whittier Birthday Book.* Extracts from the Author's writings, with Portrait and Illustrations. Uniform with the "Emerson Birthday Book." Square 16mo, very choice binding, 3s. 6d.

—— *Life of.* By R. A. UNDERWOOD. Cr. 8vo, cloth, 10s. 6d.

Williams (C. F.) Tariff Laws of the United States. 8vo, 10s. 6d.

Williams (H. W.) Diseases of the Eye. 8vo, 21s.

Wills, A Few Hints on Proving, without Professional Assistance. By a PROBATE COURT OFFICIAL. 8th Edition, revised, with Forms of Wills, Residuary Accounts, &c. Fcap. 8vo, cloth limp, 1s.

Wimbledon (Viscount) Life and Times, 1628-38. By C. DALTON. 2 vols., 8vo, 30s.

Witthaus (R. A.) Medical Student's Chemistry. 8vo, 16s.

Woodbury, History of Wood Engraving. Illustrated. 8vo, 18s.

Woolsey (C. D., LL.D.) Introduction to the Study of International Law. 5th Edition, demy 8vo, 18s.

Woolson (Constance F.) See "Low's Standard Novels."

Wright (H.) Friendship of God. Portrait, &c. Crown 8vo, 6s.

Written to Order; the Journeyings of an Irresponsible Egotist. Crown 8vo, 6s.

YRIARTE (Charles) Florence: its History. Translated by C. B. PITMAN. Illustrated with 500 Engravings. Large imperial 4to, extra binding, gilt edges, 63s.; or 12 Parts, 5s. each.

History; the Medici; the Humanists; letters; arts; the Renaissance; illustrious Florentines; Etruscan art; monuments; sculpture; painting.

London:

SAMPSON LOW, MARSTON, SEARLE, & RIVINGTON,

CROWN BUILDINGS, 188, FLEET STREET, E.C.